DREAM FALL

DREAM FALL

AMY PLUM

HARPER TEEN

An Imprint of HarperCollinsPublishers

HarperTeen is an imprint of HarperCollins Publishers.

Dreamfall

www.epicreads.com

Library of Congress Control Number: 2016961159
ISBN 978-0-06-242987-2

Typography by Ray Shappell
17 18 19 20 21   PC/LSCH   10 9 8 7 6 5 4 3 2 1

First Edition

This book is dedicated to sixteen-year-old me.
And to answer her question:
Yes, your dreams are scary enough to put in a horror novel.

Even if she be not harmed, her heart may fail her in so much and so many horrors; and hereafter she may suffer—both in waking, from her nerves, and in sleep, from her dreams.

—Bram Stoker, *Dracula*

PROLOGUE

CATA

WHITE ROOM.

White lights on a white stage.

White screen lowering from the ceiling so the white-lab-coated doctor can beam her laser pointer at a giant balloonlike image of a human brain and tell us just what she plans to do with our own messed-up models.

As if we don't already know. We're neck-deep in this thing. We understand what we're signing up for.

The overload of clinical whiteness makes my vision swim. I rub my stinging eyes and try to focus. But it's stuffy in the amphitheater, and I haven't slept in about forty-eight hours. I feel my eyelids droop and my head dip as I start to nod off. *Focus, Cata.*

I shift in my chair, sit up straighter, and take a deep breath.

I inhale a toxic-smelling blend of antiseptic and new plastic, which ties my insides into a nauseated knot. But at least it's woken me up.

Okay. What did I miss? The doctor, this tiny dark-haired woman, welcomed us and introduced herself and the other doctor. He sits onstage, hunched over, with his arms crossed, next to a boy who looks embarrassed to be here. I glance down at the agenda for the names:

Qiuyue Zhu, MD, DSc, PhD, and Thomas Vesper, MD, PhD
Pasithea Sleep Epidemiology Research Facility, Radcliffe
Medical Center

I pinch the skin between my thumb and index finger to help me stay alert. Dr. Zhu is now pointing at a highlighted section of the brain and talking about the thalamus, ". . . one area affecting sleep, and the part we will be focusing on."

I glance over at Barbara: she's listening intently like she's hearing it for the first time, but we've read all of this in the paperwork the researchers sent us. I know it so well that I could probably be up there giving the presentation myself. I'm just here to sign the waiver. Along with Barbara, that is, since she agreed to be my legal guardian. Two more years until I'm officially an adult. Which is strange, since I've felt like one since I was about nine.

My eyes wander, and I look at the others in the room—this motley assembly of families whose children are so crippled by insomnia that they're as desperate as I am to try this radical new experiment. No one could possibly understand unless they had a sleep disorder themselves. They wouldn't know that being so tired during the day that you can barely function and then wide-awake at night can make you crazy. Literally.

My vision starts to blur. *Focus, Cata.* I try.

Zhu clicks to the next slide, and up comes one of those stages-of-development graphs: a baby on the left, then a small child, adolescent, adult, and an old man far to the right. Her pointer hops back and forth between child and teen. "Most of the myelination, or development, of the brain occurs between ages five and twenty." The red dot flicks east and lands squarely on the adolescent's forehead like she's hit a bull's-eye. "Most major development has plateaued and ceased between ages eighteen and twenty. And though our brains continue to develop, after this age it's mainly a question of deterioration and regeneration."

I'm sixteen. So after a couple of years, it's basically downhill. Joy.

"That is why it is important for this particular insomnia treatment—one that can actually change your brain patterns long-term—to be administered while you are young: before the brain finishes the myelination process."

Dr.—I check the agenda again—Vesper stands now and takes the mic. He's still hunching, and his eyes are really deep set. Cavernous. He looks like a vulture. A vulture who's going to be messing with my mind. Not terribly reassuring.

The vulture speaks. "Your participation will help thousands of people like yourself. A week from today you will be our partners in a major breakthrough—not only in the treatment of, but in the *cure* for sleep disorders."

Partners? More like test animals, I think, and scan the room to check out my fellow lab rats. In the front row, center, is a small boy wearing a knitted hat with earflaps and fingerless gloves to accessorize his short-sleeved shirt and shorts. It's an unseasonably hot March in Larkmont. He's writing everything down in a notebook, oblivious to his parents, who sit on either side casting worried looks at one another.

To my right there's a boy about my age, maybe a little older. His skin is light brown, and the woman sitting next to him looks like she's from India. From the way she touches his arm—lightly but protectively—it's clear that she's his mother.

The boy's got black wavy hair and is cute in a skater-boy way— if you ignore the dark circles under his eyes and the bruise on his chin. I wonder why he's here. What he's got that's bad enough to keep him from sleeping. It could be anything: OCD, depression, narcolepsy, or PTSD, like me. For the millionth time, I think of the absurdity of it all: It's not like I've survived a war or some sort of horrible disaster. My trauma is just my life . . . stretching back over the years like a fire pit I've had to cross barefoot. It wasn't until I got some distance from it—left my life, my family behind—that the doctors claim the post-traumatic stress kicked in. I think of my sister and brother, and guilt twists in my chest like a knife. I left them. With him. I can't think about that now. I look at the girl in the row in front of me.

She's blond and pale and superthin. She looks worn and drawn

4

like everyone else in the room. But with a huge dose of sadness. Her face is so empty it's like a bottomless pit swallowed her features. Her parents hover, more obvious with their protectiveness than the mother with her son. She's a girl in danger . . . of what is anyone's guess.

A boy farther to my right looks about my age. Dirty blond hair. Tanned and freckled skin. Nondescript. He fades into the background next to the flashiness of his parents, whose jet-set casual clothes and impatient expressions suggest they're missing cocktail hour at the yacht club.

There's a boy with a short-cropped Afro sitting next to a woman dressed in a brightly patterned tribal-looking dress with matching head wrap. The way they're concentrating on Vesper's words makes me wonder if they speak English. The boy looks out of place in a way only a foreigner can.

And then there are two parents sitting alone. Holding hands. Not in a loving way, but like they're trying to keep each other from falling off a cliff. Their faces are drawn. Gaunt. They are going through something bad—no question. Their child isn't with them, but they obviously belong here.

The skater boy leans over the empty seat between us and whispers, "Bet I can read your mind."

I glance back at Barbara. She and his mom are both absorbed in the presentation and have decided to ignore us.

"Go ahead. Give it a try," I whisper back.

"You're thinking, *How did I get thrown in with this room full of weirdos?*"

I can't help but smile. "You're half-right. Room full of weirdos . . . check. But I actually included myself in the freak-fest. I feel right at home here."

He reaches out his hand. "I'm Fergus."

I shake it. "Cata. What are you in here for?"

"'Insomnia stemming from narcolepsy,'" he says, using air quotes. "You?"

"Insomnia stemming from PTSD."

He nods, and looks like he wants to ask more—what *trauma* I am *post*—but is polite enough not to.

"I feel like we're in one of those twelve-step meetings. Like I should stand up and say, 'Hi, I'm Cata, and I'm an insomniac.'"

"Yeah, but instead of group hugs, we get our brains fried." This boy is funny, and I immediately feel a camaraderie.

Fergus's mom smiles apologetically and pats him on the arm. "Honey, you should really be listening."

He shrugs helplessly, but leans back in and, after a brief hesitation, whispers, "Are you scared?"

I nod. "You?"

"Shitless," he responds.

"I know . . . We could ask for adjoining beds so we can hold hands while we get our brains fried," I say, trying to act brave and flippant, and then realize how what I just said could be read. *Did I just engage in nervous flirting?* I wait for a blush, but none comes. I'm too tired to even be embarrassed.

Fergus smiles widely, apparently reading my thoughts, or an approximation of them.

"Honey," Fergus's mom says. He wiggles his fingers good-bye.

I turn my attention to the stage as the kid who was sitting next to Vesper stands and shuffles over to join him at the mic. "This is Charles," Vesper says, "the sole member of test group Alpha. He's the reason your Beta group even exists. Just three months ago, Charles was like you. Sleepless and desperate for a solution. Now he experiences full nights of sleep."

Full nights of sleep. Those words are like a drug. Too tempting to be legal. Too promising to be true. I look around. The others want it as badly as I do.

"Does anyone have a question for Charles?" Vesper asks, and the boy in the front row's hand shoots up.

"You mentioned that one of the side effects of the treatment is short-term memory loss," he asks. "How long will it last?"

"The retrograde amnesia produced by the treatment will only cause you to forget events that happened in the days or weeks before treatment," the vulture responds. "But that is short-lived, and you should regain your complete memory quickly. Charles, would you like to share how this went for you?"

The "sole member of test group Alpha" starts talking, but I'm not listening anymore. This meeting feels like a theatrical production. The white room, white lab coats, medical words, and technical images are all meant to lull us into a sense of security. *Place yourselves in our hands. We know what we're doing.*

And what, exactly, will they be doing? Well, in a few short days, they'll be laying us out in a lab, fitting our heads with electrodes, and running electrical currents through our brains until our insomnia is fried into extinction. They'll be shocking us into normalcy.

Yes, I'm scared. But if this is what I have to do to be able to sleep again, I'm ready to sign my life away.

CHAPTER 1

JAIME

I'M IN A SCENE FROM *STAR TREK*—IN THE HIGH-tech, sterile setting of the flight deck. At least, that's what it looks like from where I sit overlooking the darkened laboratory, where a computerized column rising from the center of the room flashes ominously with multicolored lights.

The door opens, and a stream of gurneys is rolled in one by one by nurses wearing light blue uniforms. The weird lighting casts their faces in shadow.

I pinch myself for the nth time for proof that this is real. I, a mere premed student, am sitting here in the world's leading sleep technology clinic, about to witness a cutting-edge experiment.

Okay, maybe it helped a bit that I'm at the top of my class at Yale. And it didn't hurt that my mom is the personal assistant for one of the clinic's biggest donors. But I count everything I get in life as a gift. There is nothing I take for granted.

Focusing on what is happening below me, I sketch the room's layout in my notebook. The nurses are carefully transferring their seven wards onto beds arranged around the column like spokes on a wheel. The column flashes like a psychotic Christmas tree and sends out a whirring electrical hum. Stenciled numbers are painted on the concrete floor next to the beds—one to seven.

The nurses bustle around prepping the patients for the doctors' arrival by attaching sensors taped all over the subjects' bodies to cords spewing from the column. As each one connects, a light changes from flashing red to stable green, until there are only a few pulsing diodes left, scattered around the pillar.

It's slightly chilly in the room. The subjects are wearing hospital-issued socks and are draped with those metallic insulated blankets designed to trap body heat. I don't realize they're conscious until one lifts her hand to drowsily scratch her nose. Then I notice small movements from the others: wiggling toes, shifting heads, a nod from one boy when a nurse whispers something to him. Their movements are slow, drugged.

I pull my gaze away from the scene taking place below and acquaint myself with the area I've been assigned. The "monitoring station" I'm seated at is on a platform raised a couple of feet above the test area, allowing me and the researchers a clear view of all seven subjects.

The thick three-ring binder in front of me bears the mouthful of a title: "Continuous Low-Current Electroconvulsive REM

Inducement Therapy: Test File." I flip it open to a page headed "Trial Parameters" and begin reading.

I'm going to have to write this all up into a paper describing my six hours of field experience, so I start taking notes:

- *seven subjects, ages thirteen to nineteen*
- *all suffer from chronic insomnia*
- *new electroconvulsive technology will be used to try to cure them*
- *trial will last five hours, fifty minutes*

That, of course, reduces a whole page of scientific explanations to four simple bullet points, but the paper is supposed to be more about my experience than explaining the experiment to my professor.

I turn the page to the in-depth explanation of the thinking behind the experiment, precedents, and a whole lot more. Holy crap, this stuff is dense. I wish I had been given access to the information before today. It would have been nice to memorize the whole file and be better prepared. But Dr. Zhu and Dr. Vesper delayed my introductory meeting until yesterday ("for security purposes"), and, even then, only gave me the barest of descriptions of the trial.

A large flat-screen monitor takes up most of my work space, and in front of it, there's an expensive-looking computer. I'm not sure what it's for, since the doctors specified that any notes I want to take with me must be written in the notebook I bought last night. I was told not to bring my laptop, and was actually asked to leave my phone at the front desk. Again "for security purposes." Which I'm guessing means they're worried I might upload this stuff to YouTube when they aren't looking.

Although I basically had to sign my life over in the confidentiality contract, I'm not complaining. Zhu and Vesper are rock stars in the sleep research world, working on cutting-edge brain studies. This trial is going to shoot them into the stratosphere of medical-world fame. Like Nobel-quality material.

The nurses are now placing IV bags on poles next to the subjects' beds and plugging the tubes into the central column. I wonder what they're for. I look under the heading "Pretrial Preparations," and note:

- *subjects received mild sedation before they were brought to lab*
- *they must remain aware until researchers speak with them individually before the trial starts*
- *IVs provide the anesthesia that will knock them out*

I note which drug they're using and read on. One of the machines they're being hooked up to is a polysomnograph. I studied up on those last night, following Dr. Zhu and Dr. Vesper's vague explanation, in my scramble to cram as much as I could. PSGs are typical equipment used in sleep studies, which monitor the subject's brain function, eye movement, muscle activity, and heart rhythm. What's not typical in this case is that this PSG will be monitoring seven subjects at the same time. This is where the high-tech column comes in.

There is a whole section for "The Tower," as it is called, which is basically the brain of the experiment. It manages the anesthesia, the electrical current, the feedback—making sure everything is equal and simultaneous.

With a computer treating the seven subjects identically, the researchers will be able to say that the conditions were the same for all of the subjects when they report their findings. Something this groundbreaking will be picked apart by critics . . . especially since it's an invasive treatment. Electroconvulsive therapy for children and teenagers is a hotly debated topic. It's even illegal in some states. Until its efficacy is confirmed, this could kick up a shit storm in the medical world, so everything about the test has to be perfect.

The door opens and in walk Dr. Zhu and Dr. Vesper. They glance around the room, their eyes flitting up to where I sit at the monitoring station. They approach the beds—Vesper hunching over as he moves; Zhu walking ramrod straight—double-checking the placement of the electrodes being attached to each subject's temples, inserting the IV needles into the backs of their hands, speaking a few words of encouragement, and giving them a squeeze of the hand and a reassuring smile.

When they finish, Dr. Vesper climbs the steps up to the monitoring station and takes his seat in front of a pair of screens. Dr. Zhu makes her way to me and leans over to switch on my giant monitor. "Good morning, Jaime," she says. I say good morning back as my screen springs to life. It is divided into seven windows with bird's-eye views of the subjects in black and white.

Three green lights glow in the upper right corner of each window. "Since you're just observing, we've put you in front of the screen that monitors each subjects' video, audio, and power feed." She gives me a slight smile. "As we explained yesterday, there's nothing really for you to do per se, but feel free to read the general file. If it seems like a quiet moment, you are welcome to ask Dr. Vesper and me questions. And, though you may take all the notes you want for your project report, you aren't to show them to anyone except your supervising professor—who we've spoken with—until our results have been published."

"You made that clear yesterday," I reassure her.

Zhu nods efficiently and takes her chair next to Vesper. "Ready to go?" she asks, and then taps on the microphone positioned next to her screen. "It is March thirty-first, and the time is seven thirteen a.m. Administering general anesthetic . . ." She types a key, and a clicking sound starts up from the Tower. ". . . now."

A couple of minutes later, Vesper announces that the subjects are unconscious and starts the electroconvulsive current.

I turn to watch the scene behind me. The only sign that anything is happening to the subjects is a slight flexing of their fingers and toes each time the current flows, which is signaled by a crackling sound . . . like static.

This happens five times before the innovative part of the test begins. In regular ECT, the electrical current is shut off after the last pulse is given. But now it is left flowing through the subjects' brains at low levels. The static continues, but quieter, becoming a background noise.

According to Zhu's running commentary, the subjects begin dropping into REM sleep . . . all except for one. After exchanging several worried looks with Vesper, Zhu walks down into the test area and watches the boy in bed seven like he's a bomb about to go off. A second later, Vesper announces, "Subject seven has entered REM."

Zhu relaxes. "Thank the gods for that," she murmurs, and, casting an appraising glance across the sleepers, returns to her chair. The researchers busy themselves staring at the screens and talking into their microphones.

In my binder, the methodology section says we have twenty minutes to go before the next phase begins, but for now, the sensors indicate that everyone is dreaming.

CHAPTER 2

CATA

FROM THE DARKNESS COMES A SOUND.

It is one that I know too well: a bare foot squelching against the bathroom floor, painting a bright red footprint on the time-cracked tiles.

I lie paralyzed on my four-poster bed, unable to do anything but listen to the footstep, and then the pause, and then the inevitable next step as the monstrous figure drags itself from the stained enamel bathtub in the room adjoining mine. Blood squishing between skinless flesh and hardwood floor.

I'm staring at the ceiling of my cavernous old bedroom, veined with mysterious lines and cracks. Open windows like staring eyes are hung with white linen curtains billowing in the night breeze, and the floors creak at the slightest weight. Like they do now as the Flayed Man steps into my bedroom.

I try to lift an arm. My fingers shake; my hand rises an inch from the mattress but that is as far as I can move it. My body is made of lead. I am helpless. Unable to run. To hide.

I grit my teeth, summoning another ounce of strength, and am able to raise my head. There he is, framed by the bathroom door, an eerie green light shining from behind him, outlining his body as it unsteadily emerges from his space into mine. Thick blood oozes from the surface of his skinless carcass, where, in places, white bone protrudes from dark red bands of muscle. The orbs of his eyes bulge horrifically—there are no lids to hide them. A hole gapes where his nose should be, and the exposed teeth of his lipless mouth protrude like a jagged row of leaning, crumbling tombstones.

He takes another step, his head drooping slightly to one side as he staggers in my direction. He points his finger at me, raising it on a trembling hand as blood sloughs from his wrist and pools on the floor beneath his arm.

I try to scream but my throat doesn't work—the choking sound I make is swallowed by the muffled terror filling the room like a fog. With renewed determination, I manage to push myself up to a sitting position and swing my leaden legs over the edge of my bed. My feet brush the floor. When I look back up, he has abruptly crossed the room and stands mere feet away.

He takes another step toward me, reaching, dripping. His bare eyeballs give him the grotesque appearance of surprise. A shrieklike groan comes from somewhere inside him, and that is the trigger that releases me from the paralyzing gravity that's been weighing me down. As I catapult myself across the room, he lunges forward and grabs me, covering my arm with blood.

Jerking away, I struggle with the knob before throwing the door open and pitching myself into the hallway. To my left, a spiral staircase leads to the ground floor, and I fling myself down it, tripping as I go, leaning against the wall for support. I glance upward and the Flayed Man, though moving at a sepulchral pace, has suddenly advanced from my bedroom door to the landing at the top of the stairs. I hurl myself toward the front door. I grab the handle and pull with all my force. Nothing happens. It's stuck.

I scream—my voice has returned—and slam myself ineffectively against the door. The Flayed Man is halfway down the stairs, leering at me, doing his shriek-groans as he leaves a trail of gore behind him. I give up on the door and glance around to see that the coat closet is ajar. It's a futile hiding place but I take it anyway.

I scramble inside, pulling the door shut behind me, and crouch down. I push myself back until I feel the wall against my shoulders.

I know he will find me. My heart constricts as long seconds of terror-laden silence tick by, and then I hear his jagged nails scratch at the door handle. It catches. The door opens. As it widens a bony hand reaches in and scrabbles around, ripping at the coats, inches from my face.

I breathe in the coppery smell of blood and shudder from its raw stench.

The groping fingers reach my skin and grab, clawing my arm

as I leap up and smash out of the closet and past the man. For some reason, I know the front door will be open now, and there it is, standing wide, waiting. I throw myself outside, running across the front porch, past the cast-iron chairs and white wooden swing and into the perfectly mown grass of the front yard. The ground is cold beneath my bare feet, and I shiver and fold my arms across my chest as I breathe in the heady smell of gardenias and wet earth.

I feel something trickling down my arm. Blood flows from the gash the Flayed Man scratched near my shoulder. A current of alarm runs hot through me.

I swing around to see him emerge from my house. There is no one around but him. No one to run to. No one to save me but myself. I cut across the lawn and up into the backyard, my feet crunching against dry pine needles as I enter the forest of evergreens that bordered our house.

The man appears at the corner of the house. I blink, and he is halfway across the backyard. The spiny leaves of the holly bushes tear my skin, leaving welts on my arms as I plunge deeper into the woods.

The Flayed Man's shriek rings out from behind me, and I hurtle up over the top of the hill and back down the other side toward the crawfish stream. I'm getting ready to jump over a rotting log when I'm suddenly blinded by a flash of light. A tremor shakes the landscape, as if a bomb exploded. I am paralyzed with my body suspended in midair, midstride, as if God pressed pause and everything froze. A full second passes, and then I unstick and land on the other side of the log. The light has disappeared, but something weird has happened. It's like I'm running inside a shimmering bubble. Inside the bubble, nothing has changed— I'm still scrambling down the hill toward the stream. But outside it I see other people . . . in other places.

A shantytown where a boy hides behind a broken window from a truck full of soldiers. A swimming pool, water green with algae, with a girl standing at its edge watching the floating body of a child. The inside of a creepy room, where someone is blindfolded and tied to a chair. A basement lit by a single, hanging bulb, a boy beneath it staring at a line of padlocked doors. A beach in what looks like a hurricane . . . torrential winds and rains and an empty bed sitting halfway out in the waves.

And, parallel to me, a field of long grass where a boy runs, limping along frantically like he too is being chased. He looks over and our eyes meet. He glances behind me and his eyes widen. As if on cue, the Flayed Man's groaning shriek rings out, blinding me with terror.

I forget the boy and run for all I'm worth until suddenly before me stands a wall of dark, empty nothingness. The forest runs right up to the edge of it. The bleeding man gives one last cry as I fling myself face-first into the wall and my world goes black.

CHAPTER 3

JAIME

THE ROOM SMELLS LIKE DEATH. NOT THAT I KNOW what death smells like exactly. But there's this kind of mix between the sanitized smell of the AIDs clinic where I did my last internship and the airlessness of the mortuary where my father was laid out. I shudder, and immediately feel like an idiot for it.

If, after med school and residency, I achieve my goal of opening a free clinic in the Detroit neighborhood I grew up in, I'll be facing much worse things than this. The results of gang violence, drug addiction, and domestic abuse will be my everyday reality. So why am I allowing an overly sanitized lab to give me the creeps?

I reopen the test manual. I need to better understand what's going on. Maybe then I won't want to make a run for it.

The section after the summary is the Alpha test report.

Seventeen-year-old Charles B went through the same trial I'm witnessing today. Picking up my pen, I note:

- *Normal sleep has five different stages that together last ninety to one hundred minutes.*
- *For this test, Zhu and Vesper broke the five stages into two groups: rapid eye movement (REM) and non–rapid eye movement (NREM).*
- *After treatment with initial high-level electrical pulses, subjects go into REM sleep and the charge is lowered and maintained at a steady level.*
- *After twenty minutes of REM, the charge is lowered even more, kicking the subjects' brains into NREM sleep.*
- *After fifty minutes of NREM, the charge is upped and they reenter REM.*
- *Repeat for five seventy-minute REM/NREM cycles*
- *After the five cycles, the brain is conditioned into repeating this in real life—outside the lab—guaranteeing the subject something close to regular sleep.*
- *For the Alpha subject, this was a success.*
- *The results are to be verified by repeating the Alpha test identically using multiple subjects with varying sleep issues in a Beta test.*

I look up at the monitor. The subjects are in the first sleep cycle—REM—which is supposed to last twenty minutes. So when the timer at the bottom of my screen gets to nineteen, I stop reading and put the file down.

Zhu and Vesper's monitors show heart rates and brain waves scribbling up and down in zigzagged charts. They seem attentive but calm. Everything is going as planned.

But at exactly nineteen minutes and thirty seconds, just before the sleepers should transition, the earth rumbles, like a subway train is passing beneath us. Then the building shakes—just a slight tremor that sends pencils rolling off desks and monitors quivering on their stands. The lights go out.

There is a second of dead quiet, and then Zhu and Vesper are all over the place—I can see them in the green glow of the safety lights, cursing and flipping switches. But even though our screens are dark, the Tower remains unaffected: its lights are steady, and the humming and beeping of its monitors uninterrupted.

"Thank God for the backup generator." Vesper's low voice rumbles in the dark.

A clicking noise comes from the Tower, and Zhu breathes a sigh of relief. "The current decreased. They'll transition into the NREM sleep cycle. We're still on track."

And then the earthquake hits again, harder this time, and the Tower goes silent and dark. Even the safety lights are extinguished, and the room is plunged into pitch-black nothingness.

Seven mind-numbing seconds pass. Then there is a booming sound like a cannon; the lights flick on and the machines start back up.

And, all at once, the bodies of the trial subjects convulse, their arms and legs flying up in a motion that looks freakily like they're jumping through the air, before their limbs go limp and fall back onto the beds. Zhu and Vesper stare at the scene in horror, then throw themselves in front of their computers and begin frantically studying the feedback on their screens.

"Heart rates spiking," Zhu says.

"Erratic eye movements intensified," Vesper says, his already-deep voice a full pitch lower. "Breathing uneven. Brain-wave activity in gamma and rising off the charts!"

Lights start flashing red, and several of the even-paced beeps accelerate into high-pitched whines.

Zhu turns to Vesper, eyes wide, and says, "Wake them up. Now!"

CHAPTER 4

FERGUS

I AWAKE IN A COLD SWEAT. I'M SO DISORIENTED that I don't even know where I am for the first few seconds, and then I realize . . . I was just dreaming. I raise my arm to check my tattoo—my go-to for immediate comfort—but I can't see anything. It's pitch-dark in my room. I reach for my bedside lamp and then realize I'm standing.

My eyes are open and I am in complete darkness. What. The. Hell.

I listen for the typical nighttime noises: the splashing of the swimming pool fountain, the ticking of the grandfather clock in the hallway, the various vehicle and animal sounds that compose the sound track to my life in the Connecticut suburbs. But it's dead silent.

Am I still dreaming? I squeeze my arm, pinching the flesh

between my fingertips. It feels totally real.

And then the strangeness of my nightmare comes back to me. It was my lobotomy dream—the one that starts with my father telling me what a failure I am and that he's scheduled me for brain surgery, and ends with him saying he's going to do it himself and chasing me with an ice pick. Not terribly original, I know. I've watched way too many horror movies. But this dream has stuck in my psyche and now plays on regular repeat.

Except this time weird shit was happening that never had before. I fell and twisted my ankle, and Dad actually caught up with me and stabbed me in the shoulder. And it hurt like hell. I touched it, and my fingers came back dripping with warm blood. Like so hyperrealistic I could practically smell it. And I had to push myself up and run for my life to get away from him, limping awkwardly because my ankle was blazing with red-hot pain.

Then there was this flash of light, everything froze, and when it unfroze I had a window into all of these other places. In one of them, I saw this girl running away from a monster.

I hesitate, feeling a tug of déjà vu. I could swear I've seen her before. But that thought quickly evaporates as I remember what came next.

This black wall appeared in front of me—like a curtain stretching from the ground up so high it met the sky. I looked back: my father was still chasing me, ice pick raised, eyes rolled back into his head. I turned and ran for the darkness—plunged straight into it—and woke up here.

That was the most lifelike dream I have ever had, and I've

had some vivid ones, especially if you count the hallucinations that come as a bonus prize with my narcolepsy. I force myself to switch channels from *What the Hell Was That About?* to *Where Am I Now?* Fighting the mounting fear that something is very wrong (*Stay calm, Fergus*), I shuffle blindly forward, groping in the darkness to feel out the room I'm in, but there is nothing to touch. I crouch down and place my hands near my feet. Even the ground is unreadable: not cold, not warm, just hard and smooth, like glass.

I'm no longer in my lobotomy dream. I'm not in my home. Where am I? Did I spend the night somewhere else? I try to think back to what I did last night before going to bed. My mind is blank. I can't remember anything before the nightmare. I mean, I remember my mom and dad, of course. The fact that I'm in my first year of college. The fight I had with them about wanting to live away from home and Dr. Patterson taking their side, saying it was "too dangerous" for someone with my "condition."

My condition. This must have something to do with the narcolepsy. I must have passed out somewhere and hit my head hard enough to knock myself unconscious. It's happened before, but it's never given me amnesia—at least those times I remembered how I got there. But where could I be?

Something moves in the darkness. A slow, slithering sound. I freeze, a coil of fear twisting in my stomach. I'm torn between calling out and staying silent, and opt for the latter—whatever it was, it didn't sound human.

Then, from another direction comes a rhythmic tapping

noise: *tap tap tap tap*, long pause, *tap tap tap tap*, long pause. My face turns ice-cold. *Don't freak out*, I think, wishing I could see my tattoo. *It's just the hallucinations signaling you're about to fall asleep again.* The tapping continues, and I leap away from it, plunging blindly into the darkness.

From somewhere close comes a girl's voice. "Hello?" It's barely a squeak—she sounds terrified.

"Who's there?" I ask.

There is a pause, then the voice responds, "Cata." I whip around and grope in the direction it came from. Nothing. A bodiless voice. *You're hallucinating.* Dread creeps a slimy path up my back. And then something brushes my arm.

I jump, and whatever it is shrieks, "What is that?" It's a girl's voice, but not the same as the first. This voice is lower, and comes between sobs. "Oh my God, where am I?"

And then a light flickers on in front of me. Not one light, but several. Four glowing blue lines in the shape of a door, floating in the void. I glance around to see if anything else is illuminated by its glow, and notice the faint outline of two girls, one on either side of me, a few feet away.

Suddenly, a loud, hollow knock comes from somewhere above. Then another. And, as the door creaks open, I feel my stomach drop. I hear screams from the girls as a third and final knock sweeps me off my feet and high into the air, spinning me inside an invisible vortex and through the door. In a blinding flash of light, we are gone.

CHAPTER 5

JAIME

BY THE TIME ZHU AND VESPER GET TO THE SLEEP-
ers, the beeps reach a screeching crescendo and then stop. There
is a split second of silence, and then the red lights suddenly switch
to green, and the beeping restarts at the normal tempo.

The researchers look at each other, and then at the small
screens on the Tower. "Heart rates and breathing have stabilized," Vesper says.

"Except Beta subject seven," Zhu corrects him. "His have
remained elevated."

"He's our wild card. We have to regard his feedback separately,"
Vesper comments, leaning forward to inspect that monitor.
"You're the one who made the point that he's not even in the
same league as the others."

"We need to wake them up anyway," Zhu urges.

I can't bear just sitting here. "Can I do anything?" I call, my voice trembling. But the researchers either don't hear me or don't want to.

I watch, electrified, as Zhu and Vesper try to wake the subjects.

Zhu takes the girl on bed one by the shoulders and shakes her gently. "Catalina?" she says. "You need to wake up."

Vesper goes to bed two and begins slapping the boy's hand with his fingertips. "Fergus," he says, leaning in toward his face. No response.

Zhu whips around and meets my eyes. "Jaime, go to my computer. Now."

I leap from my seat and scramble to her workstation.

"Do you see the window open in the top right corner of my screen?"

"Yes," I say, and, grabbing the mouse, run the cursor up to a window labeled "ECT."

"Pull the toggle at the bottom of the window from green to red."

I do it, and the low hum from the Tower stops.

"Now pick up the phone, dial nine, and ask the operator to send emergency medical responders immediately to the basement laboratory in building one."

I make the call, trying to keep my voice from shaking.

The paramedics arrive—a team of four—and as the doctors hurriedly explain what happened, they begin inspecting the kids, opening eyelids and shining lights in their eyes, taking pulses, inspecting the feedback on the Tower monitors.

"I'll attempt waking with ammonia," one of them says, and holds a vial under subject one's nose. No reaction.

"Their breathing and heart rates are stable," says another, "so it wouldn't make sense to employ lifesaving techniques."

Lifesaving techniques? For some reason, my thoughts go to the parents who are somewhere outside, waiting for their children. When will they be notified?

The EMTs talk about setting up life-support machines in the room, "in case conditions deteriorate." As they make their exit, Zhu and Vesper work their way around the room, removing the subjects' electrodes but leaving all of the sensors connected for monitoring.

I slip back into my spot, and once again it's like I don't exist. Which I actually prefer. Something awful has happened, but I don't have enough information to grasp the scope of it. And the feeling of not knowing . . . of having absolutely zero control over the outcome . . . is making me feel panicky. My stomach twists with anxiety as my eyes flit from the researchers to the subjects and back.

Zhu and Vesper have returned to their chairs. "Brain waves are primarily delta," Vesper says. "No mental activity. We have to call it what it is and care for them accordingly in the hope that something changes."

Zhu stares at the monitors like she's in a trance. Finally, she leans toward her microphone. "With the assistance of a team of paramedics, Dr. Vesper and I attempted to awaken the subjects, but none regained consciousness."

Vesper is staring at her like he's challenging her to do something impossible. "Call it," he urges.

She sighs and says, "As of seven fifty-five a.m., I declare all seven subjects comatose."

CHAPTER 6

CATA

I AM SUCKED FROM THAT PLACE OF DARKNESS, with the disembodied voices and terrible knocking, through a glowing blue door, and find myself plunged into a dark liquid. It happens so suddenly that I don't even struggle—I stay suspended for what feels like an entire minute, not understanding what's happened until I breathe in through my nose and begin choking.

And then my reflexes kick in and I raise my arms to execute a powerful upward stroke while scissoring my legs. My head breaks the surface and I am gasping and sputtering and tasting brine . . . not brine, but something fishy and foul. I tread to stay afloat and find that I'm not swimming in water. It's something warm and thick, like mucus. *I'm swimming in liquid snot,* I think. I gag and spit and blow it out of my nose. My shoes are heavy, dragging me down. Holding my breath, I go under and yank one off, and then the other, letting them float away as I fight my way back up. I fill my lungs with air, and then, wiping the stuff from my eyes, I try to get my bearings.

I'm in a cave. The walls are wet with slime, and there's the sound of dripping, echoing, *slop . . . slop* as the thick liquid leaks from a ceiling high above me into the lake. I turn myself in a circle, investigating the space.

It is an immense room filled with the sludgy sea—the only dry land being a shelf of rock emerging from the lake to form a type of shoreline along the wall in front of me. On the far ends of the space to my left and right, tunnel-like openings suggest that this is only one section in a series of caverns.

The murky light is barely enough for me to see the entire room, and I can't tell where it's coming from. The walls? The lake itself? A green phosphorescent mist hangs above the surface of the lake.

I propel myself toward dry land, nauseated from the sensation of the gluey substance sliding past my skin. As I near the shore, I catch sight of something . . . someone already there, crouching against the wall in the shadows. I freeze, my heart seizing in fear. I don't know whether I should keep swimming toward it or away. And then I see a pair of pink Converse tennis shoes. It's a person, not a monster. Not the Flayed Man.

I kick and paddle toward the shore, and the person leans forward, tipping her head to see me better. "Hello!" I call. She unfolds and walks toward the edge of the water. Standing before me is a painfully thin girl with long, blond hair, dressed in skinny jeans and a long-sleeved loose top. Her clothes are dry.

She obviously didn't land in the slime like I did. So how did she get there? How'd *I* get here, for that matter?

The girl is silent, watching as I make my way toward her, and then calls, "Are you real?" I recognize her voice. She's the one who was crying in the blackness, just before we got sucked into this cave.

I don't answer—I'm using all of my strength to move my arms and legs to propel myself through this thick, nasty liquid. My bare feet scrape the ground. It's solid rock, but so slippery and slimy that I paddle a few more strokes before I stand and carefully wade the short distance to shore.

The girl must have decided I'm real. She waits for me, arms wrapped protectively around herself. And then something behind me seizes her attention and her hands fly to her mouth. With eyes like saucers, she shrieks, "Watch out!"

Something grabs my ankle and yanks me back as my body pitches forward. My chin hits the rock with a loud crunch, and I am dragged under the liquid. Pain shoots up through my jaw and my lungs scream for air as I struggle to claw my way up. The grip on my ankle tightens, and I kick at it as I lift my head above the liquid to gasp in some oxygen.

"Grab my hand!" I hear, and grapple forward to where the blond girl stands knee-deep in the slime, her arm stretched toward me. I kick hard again, my foot connecting sharply with whatever is shackling me. Its grasp is broken as I thrust my body forward to reach for the girl's hand. She pulls hard, dragging me forward on my knees, jagged rocks cutting into my skin as I scramble onto the rock shelf.

We both scuttle backward to the cave wall, but whatever is in the water doesn't come out. I hack and cough and spit out the foul-tasting liquid, wiping a trail of dark green slime on the back of my hand. "What was that?" I ask, panting.

Her eyes glued to the water, she responds, "Blue. It was this sick kind of blue. It looked kind of like that Gollum thing, you know, from *Lord of the Rings*." She turns to me, her face strained with fear. "Are you the girl from that dark place before? Cata?"

I nod. "I heard you too," I say. "You were . . ." I almost say *crying*, but she looks like she's about to start again. ". . . you were there. And there was a boy."

"I'm BethAnn." The way she says it—like it's of utmost importance—it's like she thinks that by naming herself she can make some sense out of the horrific world we're trapped in. She points to my face. "You're bleeding."

I touch my chin, and my fingers come away smeared in blood. Holes are torn in my sopping-wet jeans, and through them I see my knees are bleeding too.

"Oh my God, there's someone else out there," BethAnn says, pointing to the middle of the lake. Barely visible in the glowing mist, a boy swims toward us, cutting his way through the murky slime. I squint through the gloom, and, as he gets closer, I recognize him. I've seen him before. He's the one who was limping through the field of high grass as I was running from the Flayed Man.

"Watch out!" I yell to him. "There's something in there!"

The boy is swimming like I had, dog-paddling to keep his head above the slime. But, hearing my warning, he throws himself forward into a practiced crawl, cutting his way through the lake at an impressive pace. He gets about ten feet from the shore before being jerked under the surface.

"We have to help him!" BethAnn screams.

The two of us run to the water's edge, looking at each other as if daring the other to take the plunge. I look back out over the lake, squinting to try to see through the green haze. He hasn't resurfaced. No matter how terrified I am, I can't just let this guy drown.

"I haven't swum in three years," BethAnn pleads, her voice trembling.

So, it's up to me. Swallowing my fear, I scan the surface of the lake for the Gollum before venturing back into the liquid. I'm a few steps out when I lose my footing on the slippery rock and pitch backward, landing hard on my butt. Stars flash behind my eyes as pain shoots up my tailbone.

I hear a splash. BethAnn seems to have overcome her fear of swimming: she's plunged into the lake and is paddling out toward where the boy went under.

Wincing, I use my hands to get up and wade carefully toward them. A seaweed-type sludge drips from my fingers, and I flick it away while scanning the lake. I can't see a thing under the surface.

And then, a few yards from me, there is an eruption of bubbles. I struggle out toward it as BethAnn emerges from the slime, spitting and gasping as she gains her footing. "I got him," she yells. I wade forward and, bracing myself, grasp her arm and pull with all my might.

As she rises from the murk, the boy's head breaks the surface behind her. He coughs and gasps for breath. We each take an arm and pull him, fighting against the invisible force dragging him in the other direction. The boy thrashes, kicking hard, and the pressure releases so abruptly that the three of us lurch backward into the slime. And then we're scrambling and slipping and clawing our way out until we're on the shore, retreating to the back of the rock shelf, as far as we can from the toxic lake.

"What. The fuck. Was that?" the boy gasps. He and BethAnn are coughing and spitting and taking in great lungfuls of air.

"Are you the guy from the dark place?" BethAnn asks. She seems oddly obsessed with sorting out the details, seeing that she just escaped being dragged into a slime lake by an unseen monster.

The boy nods. "Fergus," he gasps.

"BethAnn," she responds. For a moment she seems reassured. But her eyes flit to the lake and she lets out a bloodcurdling scream. I turn toward where she's looking. There is a ripple in the liquid at the edge of the lake. A hand emerges, clawing at the rock.

CHAPTER 7

FERGUS

FIRST IT'S JUST A HAND. A BLUE HAND—THE GRAY-
ish blue of a corpse. And then a second hand emerges from the
lake, scraping at the rock shelf with grotesque jagged claws as
the monster drags its hideous form out of the lake. A bald head
emerges, skin stretched tight over an elongated skull. Its bulbous
eyes blink at us, see-through vertical lids flicking inward and outward. A skeletal body follows, its protruding spine curved and
crested. It hunches over and oozes mucus as it inches toward us.

The blond girl . . . BethAnn . . . grabs my arm and clutches me
so tightly that her fingernails bite into my skin. "Oh my God, oh
my God," she chants, wheezing with fear. The dark-haired girl is
on my other side, and is silently backing away.

The thing is out of the water now and crawls slowly on all
fours, its head raised, blinking obscenely at us. It looks like it

crawled straight out of a horror film, but no effects team could create something this gruesome. Its mouth hangs open, and green slime drips from pointed white teeth as sharp as blades. Terror chokes me. I feel my head nod forward and my knees grow weak. *No, not now!* I grab my forearm and focus on my tattoo: "DFF" inked in curly Gothic letters. I breathe in deeply and feel my strength return.

I have to calm myself so I won't get too emotional and collapse. Surely something I've seen is scarier than this, I reason. How about *The Ring*? The Japanese version. That was terrifying, and I watched it so many times it made me yawn. I glance back at the monster, and it slowly lifts its head to look me in the eyes, and I'm paralyzed by shock and confusion. Although the grotesque features mask any sense of humanity, there is something there that strikes a chord deep in me. For a moment, I have the craziest feeling that something is familiar about the creature. Something is familiar about all of this.

Then I recognize the creature's eyes. They're the same cold green shot through with brown as my dad's. And they're staring straight into my own. I shudder with horror and disgust.

"What do we do?" BethAnn shrieks, shaking me from the illusion. I look back and those eyes are set in the face of a monster. It is not my dad. But I've been here before. I can feel it—a memory that is just beyond my grasp.

I yank my mind from the sense of déjà vu and force it into strategy mode. We're trapped. If we stay here, the monster's got us. If we go back in the lake, it could follow us. Or, scarier still, there could be more of them lurking below. Waiting to grab us with their bony fingers and pull us under.

I glance around at the shelf we're standing on, trying to spot anything I can use as a weapon. There's nothing growing inside the cave. No branches or roots to break off and use. But, a few yards away in the shadows, a section of the ceiling has caved in, and large pointed stones—stalactites?—are piled in a spiky mound below. The brown-haired girl has noticed them too, and makes a dash toward them. BethAnn is clinging to me so ferociously, I'm pretty much immobilized. By the time I'm able to disentangle myself, the brunette is already rummaging through the stones. She picks one up, but it slips through her fingers and shatters against the floor.

She lunges for another and comes out with a shard the size of a baseball bat. Holding it in both hands, she strides toward the monster. It is halfway across the shelf, crawling like a spider toward BethAnn, who is screaming like she's the victim in a slasher movie.

I've made my way to the rock pile, and, leaning down to grab the heaviest one I can find, I head back toward where the girl has confronted the monster. The gruesome creature has seen her coming and switches into high gear, scrambling toward her faster than she can move out of the way. And then it pauses midattack and directs its attention to me, staring unblinkingly with my father's eyes.

I hear him speak. "Your illness is a figment of your imagination. You could heal yourself if you wanted, but you don't want to be normal, do you? You're pathetic." The voice seems to come from the direction of the beast, dripping poison into my ears with those words I know so well.

The girl takes advantage of the creature's being distracted and raises the rock shard high over her head.

"Wait!" I yell without thinking. She hesitates, then watches in horror as it dives for her leg and clamps its claw around her ankle.

I fumble forward, numb with shock. *What the hell, Fergus? This monster is not your dad.*

The girl is kicking at it. She stumbles backward and loses her grasp on her stone, which clatters to the floor. I pull my arm back to lance mine like a spear, but the girl is in my way now, and I'm afraid I'll hit her.

The creature grabs her ankle with its other claw, and as it throws its head back to bare its teeth, I finally have a clear shot. I hurl my stone, and it connects with the monster's protruding rib cage. Its scream is a chilling mix of a baby's cry and a raven's croak, amplified to a deafening level by the cave's acoustics. It lets go of the girl's ankle.

BethAnn darts forward, picks up the rock shard the other girl dropped, and swings it high over her head. She brings the stone down with a powerful blow, smashing the beast's head so hard that the stone embeds in its skull. She lets go and scuttles away as I grab the brunette under her arms and pull her toward me. The monster lies lifeless on the ground, dark goo oozing from under the stone forming a gelatinous puddle around the head.

I want to throw up, but it's not because of the gore. It's because

I have this totally irrational feeling that we just bashed in my father's head.

What is wrong with me? That wasn't my father. It was a freaky blue monster. A monster that was trying to kill us.

You're always having dreams about your dad trying to kill you. The thought zigzags through my brain like a lightning bolt. *Dream. This is your dream. And you've been here before.*

"Is it dead?" BethAnn calls. Now that her moment of glory is over, she's cowering a few feet away, hands clenched into fists.

"Looks dead, but who knows," I respond, trying to keep my voice calm. "We have to get out of here."

The brown-haired girl stands there, zoned out, staring at the monster.

"Are you okay, Cata?" yells BethAnn. "Did it hurt you?"

The girl, Cata, shakes her head like she's coming out of a daze. "I'm okay." She looks at BethAnn, and then at me, her blank expression melting into a scowl. "Why did you tell me to wait? I had it!"

"I don't know," I say. "Something felt . . . wrong." I don't want to tell them we're in my dream. It sounds too crazy. And besides, even though I know I've been here before, I have no idea what could happen next.

She shoots me the stink-eye, then turns back to BethAnn. "Thanks for saving me."

"No one's safe yet," I cut in. "We have to move."

"Where?" BethAnn asks, looking around like she expects to see an exit sign hanging on the wall.

"Looks like there are two ways out," I say, pointing to the tunnels on either side of the room.

"You mean get back in the water?" BethAnn asks, horrified.

Cata forgets that she's pissed with me and looks out doubtfully over the lake. "I guess it's either that or just wait here and see what else comes out of the slime."

"There might not be any more of those things," BethAnn says. "And if there are, we can defend ourselves better on dry land than swimming in that . . . stuff."

Cata looks back down at the dead monster and shakes her head. "We have to get out."

"Maybe we should just stay here, where it's safe," BethAnn insists.

The words are barely out of her mouth when it seems like the entire ceiling detaches and swoops down upon us in a suffocating cloud of wings and claws.

"Bats!" Cata screams, and crouches over, swatting them out of her hair.

She's only partially right. The body and wings are those of bats, but the heads look exactly like the creature we just killed. Flying monsters with my dad's eyes. What. The. Fuck. I definitely don't remember ever seeing this before. There are dozens of them swarming all over me, scratching my face and my arms with their claws. My dad whispers, "You choose to remain a prisoner of your own mind."

"Get out of my head!" I growl back, then turn, yelling, "Into the lake!"

I can't even see the girls, the cloud of bats is so thick, but as I make a run for the lake and plunge into its nasty slime, I hear two splashes behind me, one after the other. I dive under the surface, squeezing my eyes shut, and swim a few strokes through the phlegmy liquid before coming up for air. I wipe the goo from my eyes and look around. The girls are right behind me, swimming with panicked strokes away from the bat creatures, who have landed on the shelf, having given up the chase as soon as we entered the water.

"Which way do we go?" asks Cata, holding her head above the slime, though her hair is drenched in it.

A bone-chilling animal shriek comes from the tunnel farthest from us. "Away from that!" I respond, turning to head for the closest tunnel. We swim toward its opening like our lives depend on it. Which, all things considered, they probably do.

As we near the passageway out of the cavern, I look back to the far side of the room where the noise came from. Something is taking form inside that tunnel entrance, and even though it's practically a football field away, I can tell what it is: an army of the blue lake creatures, heads bobbing horrifically above the surface of the slime as they enter the room.

"Swim faster," I yell. "We're almost out of here."

The lake has risen by the time we reach the tunnel, the slime lapping against the underside of the arch. "We'll have to dive under to the other side!" Cata yells.

"How long is the tunnel? Can we swim that far without air?" BethAnn gasps from beside me.

A chorus of shrieks come from behind us. Closer.

"No choice," I say.

She meets my eyes, and her own look deranged with fear.

"We'll do it together," I say, looking over at Cata.

She nods her agreement. "On the count of three," she says. "One . . . two . . ."

I inhale deeply, filling my lungs with the putrid air. Then, grabbing BethAnn's hand, I dive, swimming blindly, eyes squeezed shut, for what seems like an eternity. I feel her hand tugging mine, and we surface, only to find ourselves trapped in the top of the archway, only a few inches of air between us and the curved stone. "Breathe in!" I gasp. "We're almost there." I hear her sputtering and gasping beside me, before she squeezes my hand and we submerge once more. I wonder if Cata has made it to the other side, and then wonder what we'll do if she hasn't. My lungs are burning from the lack of oxygen when BethAnn pulls on my hand once again, and we surface, sputtering and wheezing and spitting the nasty liquid from our mouths and wiping it from our eyes. We're in another room, larger than the one we started in.

To our right, Cata surfaces, flailing as she slaps her hands on the surface of the lake, testing to make sure she's out of the tunnel, before wiping her eyes and looking around. "We made it," she gasps, treading hard to stay afloat.

I peer through the low light around the room. On another rock shelf, not far away, are four people—human people—staring at us like they can't believe their eyes. At their feet lie two dead monsters, identical to the one we killed.

"Help us!" BethAnn yells. "There are more of those things coming!"

A cawlike cry comes from the tunnel behind us. I swim as fast as I can, fear propelling me forward until I am close to shore and the people step down into the liquid to help drag me and the girls out. One of their group—a small boy wearing a knit hat—is sprawled on the ground with blood oozing out of a huge bite mark on his leg.

I'm wiping the foul slime out of my eyes when I turn and see the first of the grotesque heads emerge from our side of the tunnel.

"Here they come," says Cata.

Then, as we watch, something appears between the monsters and us. It looks vaguely human, but it's flickering in and out like static on an old TV screen. And it's walking on the surface of the water. Toward us.

BethAnn gives this kind of half shriek, half scream, and then from all around us comes a booming noise, like someone banging on a giant door. Everyone stares at one another, frozen in confusion.

Another bang comes, and this time I know what it is. It's the noise I heard right before I left the dark place and was plunged into the slimy lake.

A third knock comes, and a black wall opens beside us, stretching far above and below the limits of the cave. A wind whips around us, dislodging dirt from the cave floor and lifting it into a swirling cloud of dust.

As another shriek comes from the water we run full speed toward the darkness, two of the kids scooping up the hurt boy and dragging him between them.

As we plunge through the wall, the cave disappears, the wind stops, and we are back in the silent blackness where we started.

CHAPTER 8

JAIME

IT SEEMS LIKE THE RESEARCHERS ARE STALLING. They record everything that happened in meticulous detail, talking into their microphones and typing furiously on their laptops. I suspect it's not just for the sake of faithful record-keeping, but because they're dreading what comes next: telling the parents—and the rest of the world—what happened.

They haven't asked me to leave yet, so I'm guessing they hope that this can still turn around, that the sleepers will awake on their own.

I do my best to stay inconspicuous in case they've actually just forgotten that I'm here. It would probably be the right thing, under the circumstances, for me to offer to leave. But I want to see what happens.

My eyes flick up to the monitor, where seven bodies lie

motionless on their beds. Seven lives have been affected—possibly permanently—by a fluke of nature. Who are these kids? What kind of problems do they have that would prompt them—and their parents—to agree to such a risky experiment?

Glancing back to make sure the researchers are still absorbed in their work, I flip through my binder, turning pages as quietly as I can, until I get to the section with the subject files. It takes up half the binder. I might not get the time to read all the way through, but I'm suddenly desperate to attach real lives to the anonymous people lying below me. A strange emotion thrumming in my chest, I turn the page and start with trial subject one.

Her name is Catalina Cordova. She's sixteen. Her official diagnosis is post-traumatic stress disorder. There are a few pages of background history written by a psychiatrist. I skim through them, picking up phrases like "abusive father," "domestic violence," "death of mother," "petition filed for emancipation of minor." I find a section entitled "legal guardian." It states that Catalina was made a ward of the state eight months ago and is living with a friend of her late mother's.

The last paragraph summarizes why she's here. "Night terrors, resulting in chronic insomnia. Medication and counseling have failed to ameliorate her condition. A more radical therapy is suggested in order to avoid debilitating mental breakdown and permit possible future participation in a regular school situation instead of continuing her current homeschooled status."

I glance up at my screen at the window labeled "1" and look at the girl. Dark hair. Tall. Pretty, or at least as she appears so in black and white on a pixelated screen. Whatever she experienced in her past must have been bad if she was willing to go through all this in order to sleep.

Although my dad died when I was twelve, I still had a reasonably good childhood. I mean, it hasn't always been easy, but the mild bullying I had to put up with is nothing compared to violence at home. To having the person who is supposed to protect you turn out to be the one who hurts you.

I flip back to the first page, preparing to read her psychiatrist's notes from beginning to end, when something happens on the researchers' monitors. The feedback has been showing stable (meaning no) activity. Now it's kicking into high gear.

"Eye movement and heart rates are spiking," Vesper says.

Zhu leaps up to stand behind him, leaning forward to inspect his monitor. She points to a window with rows of numbers scrolling down it. "Sensors show a decrease in skeletal muscle tension."

The two doctors watch the readouts, breathless. "It looks like they're dreaming," Zhu says, "but that's impossible—their brain activity is primarily delta." After another moment of staring at Vesper's screen, she turns and walks down the stairs to the sleepers. "It doesn't make sense." She picks up one of their limp hands and taps it softly with her fingertips. "What are their bodies reacting to? They're comatose."

"I see some low-level theta waves," Vesper says, leaning forward and tracing the screen with his finger. "They *could* be dreaming."

"No way are they dreaming," Zhu retorts, clenching her hands behind her back as she leans in to inspect the screens embedded in the Tower. "Their bodies could still be responding to the abrupt interruption in electric flow. They were left without electrical current for *seven seconds* before it kicked back in. *Anything* could have happened inside their minds. There's no way we can know."

Vesper swivels his chair to look at her. He leans forward, resting his elbows on his knees. "Qiuyue, we can't just wait around for them to wake up on their own. We have to do something."

Zhu suddenly remembers that I'm there. "Jaime, I have no idea what is going to happen today. If you want, you can leave."

Although I felt like getting the hell out of here earlier, there's no way I want to go now. This isn't my experiment: I won't get any credit or blame. But I was here when it started, I was here when catastrophe struck, and I want to see it through to the end, whatever that turns out to be.

And even though I don't know these kids from Adam, if the rest of their stories are anything like subject one—Catalina's— I want them to have a second chance at a normal life. I chose medicine to help people. Not to abandon them when things look hopeless.

"If it's okay with you, I'd like to stay," I say as evenly as I can. "If there's nothing I can help you with, I'm happy to observe. I'm supposed to do at least six hours of field experience. This should count, even if you don't get the outcome you were expecting."

A look of despair passes between the two researchers. This is far from the outcome they were expecting. Zhu raises an eyebrow in question, and Vesper nods. She looks back at me. "You can stay while we are waiting for conditions to change. But if we have to

call the paramedics again—if we get into a lifesaving situation—
you will need to leave."

"I understand," I say. "Thank you." I try to disappear again,
hunching over my workstation and pretending to immerse myself
in the test file.

Zhu and Vesper start discussing different experts they can
consult. Vesper pulls out a cell phone and makes a call. He begins
explaining the situation to someone he calls "Murphy."

Zhu lets him talk a long time before interrupting him. She
points to her screen. "Look. Eye, heart, and muscle activity have
all lowered and returned to normal. We're back to where we were
fifty minutes ago."

"Besides subject seven," Vesper adds. "He's staying at the
heightened feedback."

Zhu shakes her head in futility. Vesper closes his eyes and
sighs, then continues his conversation with Murphy, reading him
statistics from his screen. He hangs up and says, "Murphy says
he would pull the plug on the test. Move them all to their own
rooms in the ICU."

Zhu is indignant. "What? He would move them? Why?
They're fine here. It's better if we can keep an eye on all of them
together. I am not giving up on these kids. Or on this test. I still
think this can turn around, even if it means taking unforeseen
action."

"What kind of unforeseen action?" Vesper asks.

"Repeating the electrical pulses, but at a higher level," she
responds, blank-faced.

"Do you know what you're suggesting?" Vesper asks in disbelief. "Basically shocking their brains out of a coma? You can't just jump-start a brain like you can a heart. We're not working with a defibrillator here. We're working with an electric current that could easily give seven teenagers permanent brain damage if we do it wrong."

"Or they could remain in comas if we don't do anything," Zhu responds. She hesitates. "There *are* precedents."

"On animals," Vesper says crisply. He pulls a Kleenex out of his pocket and mops off his face—he's sweating profusely even though it's chilly in here. He peers at the clock on his desk. "We've given it enough time. We have to tell Mike."

Zhu sighs and throws a glance behind her at the subjects, as if hoping their condition changed in the last few minutes. Shoulders slumping, she picks up the telephone. "Jonathan, it's Dr. Zhu. Please put me through to Mr. Osterman's office." She waits for a moment and then says, "Mike, we've got a crisis on our hands."

CHAPTER 9

CATA

IT'S LIKE IT WAS BEFORE. I'M STANDING IN PITCH-blackness. But it's different from mere blackness—it is the absence of light, sound, feeling, any sensation at all. I'm completely alone in the dark, my heart beating a million miles an hour, my breath ragged, pressure making my head feel like it's a balloon that's about to explode.

Now that I'm out of the cave, I'm suddenly overwhelmed with the horror of it. The slime, the pain, the hideous blue creature lying at my feet with its brains bashed in. Panic and nausea come in waves, crippling me, bending me over as I lock my arms across my middle. My body wants to throw up, but nothing comes out as I crouch down and heave over and over, my stomach cramping worse each time.

The nausea finally subsides, and I sit down, leaning forward, my head in my hands. Where am I? I feel like crying, but I stopped doing that years ago and don't even remember how.

And then I hear something. The same rhythmic tapping I heard the first time I was here. Four taps. A pause, and then four taps again. My heart shoots to my throat. Is it one of the blue creatures? Or what about that thing at the end, walking on water and flickering like a dying candle? Could it have followed me through the black hole into the darkness? Or does this place have its own monsters?

I sit motionless, too petrified to move, until finally I can't stand the silence any longer. "Is anyone else here?" My voice comes out all wobbly with fear.

There is one silent second. From a ways away, a voice sounding a hundred percent human says, "Yes."

And then, coming from closer, is a voice I recognize. "Cata, is that you?" It's the boy from the cave. Fergus.

"Yes, it's me," I respond, scrambling to my feet and groping, hands held up in front of me, toward his voice.

"Over here," he says. I reach forward and grab an arm. We fumble around until I'm clenching his hand in one of mine and clamping his arm in a death grip with the other. Just having that contact, that support, makes me dizzy with relief.

"Are you okay?" His voice is low. Calm.

"I think so," I whisper back.

"I wish there were light," says a small voice, and as soon as the words are spoken, the place is flooded with light. It's not blinding, but I shade my eyes while they adjust. The pervasive glow illuminates the space we're standing in—a space with no visible ceiling or walls, or even shadows. Just a sort of blank whiteness as far as I can see. Fergus stands beside me, and now that we are visible we drop hands.

I finally get a good look at him, slime-free, and get that feeling again like I know him from somewhere else. Somewhere outside this place. He's really tall and has chin-length ink-black hair, jade-green eyes, and his skin is the same light brown as mine. He's handsome in a skater-boy kind of way, although judging from his super-serious look, I'm sure he'd hate that description.

Skater-boy. Something tugs at my memory, but evaporates as soon as I pay attention to it.

There are other people in the space at varying distances from us. Some sit, some stand—all facing different directions. Beth-Ann scrambles to her feet, wiping tears from her cheeks. Her face is splotchy and her too-big-for-her-face blue eyes are bloodshot and swollen.

The others turn to face us. I recognize them from the cave. We walk toward each other until we're standing in an awkward circle, but no one says a word until BethAnn speaks up. Her voice is barely a whisper, but it's so quiet in the space that I can hear every word. "Are you all real?" she asks, and you can tell she's hoping we'll say no. That we're just characters in a dream and she'll wake up soon.

"About as real as *you* are, I expect," says one of the boys from the cave. Is he being snarky? But no . . . when I look at him, he has a flirty smile on his face. "After what's just happened, who knows what's real anymore?" he says and, reaching out, squeezes Beth-Ann's shoulder. She relaxes and gives him a shy smile.

The boy is almost as tall as Fergus, and has chestnut-brown hair, thick eyebrows, and piercing blue eyes. He looks a lot like that actor . . . the one from that zombie love film . . . I can't remember his name.

"Does anyone have any idea where we are?" I ask. People shake their heads.

"I've been here before," says a voice from behind me. I jump as a girl with a milky complexion, black shoulder-length hair, and straight bangs walks up and joins us. She's dressed in a black band T-shirt, a short plaid miniskirt, and fluorescent yellow tights and wears catlike eyeliner. I saw her in the cave—crouching next to the injured boy. "But last time it stayed dark."

"Same with me," says a small, wiry boy with dark skin and a foreign accent that sounds vaguely African. "I was here in the dark right before getting sucked through that door into the cave."

"Me too," says Fergus. "But before this . . . void . . . I was somewhere else. I think it was a dream . . . Actually, I'm pretty sure it's a nightmare I've had before. But at the end of it, something changed and I saw a few of you."

Everyone nods like the same thing happened to them.

"I *know* I saw you," Actor Guy says to Fergus. "And you too, I think," he says to BethAnn. "I saw you standing next to a swimming pool." The way he looks at her, he seems to be implying something, like he's protecting her from us by not mentioning the floating body I saw myself. BethAnn pales.

"Anyone else have the same experience?" Cat Eyes asks.

We all nod, and Actor Guy says, "Yeah, but I don't remember seeing you there . . . in that first place."

"Well, I saw you," she said. "You were in a basement or a storage space or something with lots of doors."

Actor Guy looks uncomfortable. He was obviously as freaked out by his nightmare as the rest of us.

She turns to the rest of us, and says in an authoritative voice, "So we were all having our own nightmares, and at the end *some* of us saw each other, and then we came here to this"—she glances at Fergus and uses air quotes, flashing a yin-yang tattoo on her wrist—"'void-y' place before getting sucked into that nightmare of a creepy cave."

This girl sounds like she's used to organizing people. Confident. Self-assured. And tough enough to be a little bit scary.

"If *nightmare*'s even the right word for it," Actor Guy says. "I've never had a bad dream as realistic as that."

"Well, dream or not, it definitely wasn't real, because Ant there"—Cat Eyes points at a boy wearing fingerless gloves and one of those South American knitted hats with earflaps—"had blood gushing from a slime monster bite, and now that we're in . . . the Void . . ." she says, considering the name she just gave this place and then nodding, satisfied, ". . . well, look."

Everyone turns to look at "Ant," who wears shorts along with his matching knitwear. He was the one sprawled on the ground in the cave, injured. Now his leg is bite-free. He diverts his eyes, obviously not enjoying the attention.

"Cata cut her chin pretty bad," says BethAnn, glancing at me. I press my fingers to it to check—no blood. I look down. The holes are gone from the knees of my jeans, which look like they just came out of the washing machine. And the shoes I kicked off to swim are back on my feet.

"We were all soaked with that green phlegm from the snot lake," comments Actor Guy. He gestures toward his jeans, which look off-the-shelf new.

Cat Eyes pinches her chin, thinking. "Individual dream, Void, collective dream, Void," she says to herself. She turns to Fergus and me, and glances over at BethAnn. "By the way, the rest of us already met in the cave. I'm George."

"*George?*" BethAnn blurts out, and then looks embarrassed.

"Short for Georgina," George says. "Got a problem with it?"

BethAnn's eyes get deer-in-headlights wide. She presses her lips together and shakes her head.

Everyone else gives their name except the foreign guy, who looks totally stressed out. "Are we really going to stand around getting to know each other, or are we going to figure out how to get out of here? Not to be rude, but I hope not to stay long enough to get acquainted."

When he speaks, it sounds like he's singing. Although his English is perfect, the accents are on all the wrong syllables, and I have to concentrate to understand.

"So where exactly are you going, *Remi?*" asks George. One hand is poised on her hip and the other tucks a strand of hair behind her ear. "I can't wait to hear your escape plan."

"I just don't see the point in wasting time making friends. I mean, *she* isn't even sure if we're real." His melodic accent doesn't hide the emotion in his words. I'm sure we're all scared here, but he seems downright shell-shocked.

"My *name* is BethAnn," she responds.

Remi just peers around the space, as if hoping another door is going to appear.

"Listen, Remi," George says. "I saved your ass from those monsters back there. If we're stuck going back and forth between this Void and those dreams, you might want to know whose name to scream next time you need to be rescued."

"It's not my fault I fell," he mumbles. Humiliated, he glances apologetically at BethAnn, who refuses to meet his gaze.

Fergus watches George's badassedness with admiration, while Zombie Actor, who introduced himself as Sinclair, stifles a laugh at Remi's embarrassment.

"Based on what went down in the cave, I wouldn't mess with George," he says, throwing her a look of complicity. "If you're smart, you'll join her team instead of trying to come up with your own plan."

He throws her a flirty wink and she frowns. "Think you might want to bring it down a notch? You already came on to me in the slime cave. Unsuccessfully."

Sinclair throws his hands up in innocence. "Whoa, whoa, whoa . . . I never came on to anyone. I was just being friendly." But the look he gives her is full-on flirtatious.

She crosses her arms. "Not interested," she says dryly.

His smile spreads, and he mimics her arm cross. "Not trying," he responds, clearly relishing the drama.

I butt in. "Um, can we skip the lovers' spat and talk about what's going on? We have no clue where we are. But it might help if we figured out how we got here."

BethAnn starts to say something, and then stops, looking unsure.

"What, BethAnn?" George prods.

"The whole time I've been here in"—she pauses—"what did you call it? The Void? I've been trying to think back to before the first nightmare—to what I did last night before going to bed. But I'm drawing a total blank."

Everyone shuts up, and you can tell we're racking our brains, trying to remember. I can't recall what I did last night either, but how about yesterday? With an empty feeling in the pit of my stomach, I realize I can't remember anything before waking up in the Flayed Man dream. I dig deeper.

Okay, I remember being taken away from home, of course. Moving in with Barbara. Too panicky to leave the house, I binge-watched DVDs for a couple of months before she insisted on enrolling me in a homeschooling program. But I can't really place how long ago that was. It feels like it could have been years ago . . . or yesterday.

George breaks the silence. "Does anyone remember what happened before that first dream? Like BethAnn said . . . where you were last night . . . what you were doing?"

There is a group shaking of heads. Worried looks.

Fergus chimes in. "Anyone know what day it is?" he asks. "Month?"

Collective silence.

Ant speaks up, his voice almost a whisper. "The last thing I remember is Christmas."

"I remember New Year's Eve," offers Sinclair with an inside-joke wag of the eyebrows—like . . . if we only knew the things he had done.

"Okay, so we're at least post–January first," Fergus says, picking up from Sinclair. "Anyone remember something later than that?"

The homeschool program began in December. I remember the geeky grad student Barbara found to tutor me during the first few weeks. Then . . . nothing. So I'm up to January. I shake my head, and so do BethAnn and George.

Remi speaks up, offering his story with a sigh, like he thinks this exercise is a waste of time. "I moved to America on February fifth. I remember that day and starting school the next week. I don't remember anything after that."

"So we all have memory loss," murmurs George.

Ant takes that as his cue to sit down. He begins tapping the floor with his finger. *Tap tap tap tap. Tap tap tap tap.*

Oh my God. It's the sound I heard in the Void the first time, and again before the lights came on! The one that scared me half to death. There's something about it that puts me on edge. I shudder.

Sinclair looks at me and, in a low voice, as if he's taking me into confidence, he says, "He kept doing that in the cave, and it nearly got him eaten." He leans toward me as he speaks, brushing my arm with his.

Wow, this guy is definitely a flirt. But it doesn't really bother me. It's been a long time since I even thought about boys, and it's actually nice to get the attention.

I make myself turn away from him and watch George sit down next to the boy. "Ant's just nervous," she says, and puts her hand on his arm.

Remi fidgets impatiently. "Ten minutes in the cave and they're already best friends. Our goal is to get out of here. Not to pamper this kid who acts like he's autistic."

Ant looks up at him and tips his head to one side, the squint of his eyes showing frustration, not the hurt you would expect to see after that kind of comment. "I'm not autistic," he says in a small voice.

George looks up and gives Remi a sour face. "You might not care about political correctness, but there *is* this thing called basic human decency. Oh, yeah, and another thing called *Don't put people in a fucking box.*"

Remi shakes his head and mutters some words under his breath. I catch *foolish* and *irresponsible*. After that I ignore him and, following George's example, sit down. One by one, so does everyone else. It feels a lot more natural than standing around in a circle.

Fergus sits a couple of feet away from me and rubs his forearm, staring at this tattoo he's got, before he looks up and around the at group. "So why are we here? It seems like we've all got memory loss back to a certain point. Does anyone know each other? I mean . . . in real life?"

Everyone shakes their heads. BethAnn says, "No, but I have a feeling I've seen a couple of you before. You seem familiar," she says to Ant. "And you." She nods at Remi. "But it's supervague. It could just be when we saw each other at the end of the first dream." She looks troubled, like she's reaching for something that's just beyond her grasp.

"Well, what do we have in common, then?" I ask. "We're all teenagers . . . I think. I mean, I'm sixteen."

"Eighteen," says Fergus, and everyone else chimes in.

BethAnn's the oldest at nineteen. Ant's the youngest at thirteen. Remi and George are both fifteen, and Sinclair is seventeen.

"Where's everyone from?" George asks. Everyone answers different states, except Remi, who says he's from Matangwe, and when that gets blank stares, he huffs, "That's in Africa. But I live with my aunt now in Minneapolis."

"Okay, we're all teenagers who *currently* live in the United States, and we all have memory loss. I doubt that information's going to get us very far," Fergus says. He looks disappointed, like he had hoped we were on to something.

"And the first thing we remember is a nightmare," says George.

"You mean the last thing," Fergus corrects her.

"The first," Ant insists quietly. He is pressing his fingers to his wrist like he's taking his pulse. Then, letting go, he taps four times on the ground and says to himself, "When working with an unknown situation, you have to identify known factors and work within their boundaries."

Everyone looks at each other in confusion.

"I think what Ant means," says George, "is that while we're here we've got to play by the rules of this world."

"See what I mean?" Remi says. "These two are already practically finishing each other's sentences. This is not the time to make friends, and it's not the time to philosophize. It's the time to strategize." He plants his gaze on George, challenging her to respond.

George looks at him like he's barely worth her time. "I think we've established that until we know more, it's going to be kind of hard to come up with a plan."

I shift uncomfortably, watching the stare-down between George and Remi. Conflict pushes all my buttons—I avoid it at all costs. BethAnn doesn't seem to be enjoying it either. She's sitting there with her arms around her legs, enveloping her undernourished frame like she's hiding a secret. *Anorexia,* I think. A girl in my old school had it, and she was always trying to hide beneath oversized tops because, even though she was skeletal, she thought she looked fat.

"Clothes." The word is out of my mouth before I know what I'm going to say. I think for a second. "Our clothes. They were wet and slimy before, like Sinclair said. And my jeans were torn. And before that, in my first nightmare I was wearing a . . ." I hesitate, but Fergus jumps in.

"You were in a white nightgown," he says, remembering.

"How Gothic romance of you," Sinclair remarks teasingly. He winks, and I can't help blushing.

"Cata has a point," George says. "If we're in a dream—"

"But we're not in a dream," BethAnn interrupts. "We're actually having a conversation." She tugs on her long, limp hair. "Everything feels as real as in the outside world."

"You just said it right there," George says, pointing to Beth-Ann. "Outside world." She looks around at us. "Whether this right now is a dream or not, it doesn't matter. We're no longer in the 'outside world.' We're somewhere else."

"A place where nightmares are always around the corner," says Sinclair spookily, waving his fingers.

"If only they were just around the corner, and not through a creepy glowing door," I say.

"Void. Nightmare . . ." murmurs Ant, tapping the ground.

"This is getting us nowhere," Remi says, squeezing his forehead in frustration.

"Listen, you guys," BethAnn says, "picking on each other isn't going to help anything. We need to work as a group if we're going to figure this out."

"Nineteen," says Ant.

Everyone stops and stares at the boy. "What?" asks Remi incredulously.

"Nineteen," he repeats, in a small firm voice.

And just then, in the center of the circle we've all formed, a wooden door appears, its edges glowing blue. A knocking sound booms from somewhere high above us.

"Not again," BethAnn says.

We scramble to our feet, all except for Ant. He buries his head in his arms, and George squats down to hug him, cocooning him with her body.

A second boom comes. The door slowly creaks open, and wind begins to whip around us.

"I don't want to go back in," BethAnn says, shrinking back from the glowing opening.

Fergus puts his arm around BethAnn. "We survived the last one. We can do this thing," I hear him murmur.

"It's always three knocks," says Sinclair. "I for one am not going without a fight." Bouncing up on his toes, he sprints away from the door into the whiteness, putting as much distance as he can between himself and us.

The third boom comes, and a bright light flashes. I feel myself being whisked up into the air and through the door. The force rips the breath from my lungs and makes my head feel like it's blowing up like a balloon. And for the second time, I am leaving the Void for who knows where.

CHAPTER 10

JAIME

TRIAL SUBJECT TWO IS NAMED FERGUS WILLSON. He's eighteen. Freshman at a local community college. His file looks a lot more medical than Catalina's, stuffed with charts and readouts and prescriptions dating back years. He's diagnosed as having narcolepsy with cataplexy, hypnagogic hallucinations, sleep paralysis, excessive daytime sleepiness, and night terrors.

I've heard of narcolepsy, of course, but don't know a couple of the other terms. I open up the search engine on the fancy computer and type in *cataplexy*. Three hundred eighty-four thousand results. Scanning a few, I see that it is a condition that about seventy percent of narcoleptics suffer where they experience sudden muscle weakness triggered by emotions. I've seen something about this before on a documentary—if the guy laughed, cried, or was frightened, he just collapsed wherever he was, sometimes injuring himself pretty badly.

The entry for "hypnagogic hallucinations" makes them sound just as bad. They happen when someone is falling asleep and are so lifelike the person isn't sure if they're real. They can involve any, or all, of the senses. Although they can occur without narcolepsy, the hallucinations are more common and severe with narcoleptics.

I click on a link where people share their experiences with these hallucinations, and read one woman's story where a huge, hairy spider was on her forehead. She not only saw it, but felt it—vividly—and since something called sleep paralysis can go hand in hand with the occurrence, she had to lie there motionless while it crawled across her face. I shudder, wondering which of the two conditions would be worse: falling down in public or being crawled on by hyperrealistic spiders.

Window number two on my monitor shows a tall boy with black hair. I check his vitals. Six four. The photo in his file shows an angry-looking guy with dark circles under his eyes. Underneath is a list of restrictions: no driving, sports, or work that involves dangerous materials. He has to live with another adult who takes responsibility for his safety in the home. In parentheses behind that clause is handwritten "lives with parents." No wonder he's angry.

The door to the lab flies open, and big man in a suit strides into the room. "Zhu. Vesper," he acknowledges as they spring to their feet. As he marches around the circle of beds, they trail along behind him, explaining what happened and kowtowing in a way that leads me to assume this is Michael Osterman, the hospital director. He leans in to inspect one of the subjects, hands clasped behind his back as he maintains a safe distance from the sleeper. Finally, he turns to the researchers. "Well, we've got messes to clean up all over the clinic, thanks to the power cutoff caused by what the news is calling 'a minor seismic event.' So I have other crises on my hands. This one is yours to handle. What do you propose?"

"We're consulting with Erwin Murphy at Mt. Sinai," Vesper says.

Osterman nods. "Good thinking. You might want to try Frankel as well."

Vesper heads for his computer, finds the number, and dials. The director glances my way but looks right through me as his gaze swings back to the researchers. Since I'm not important, I don't exist to him. Good.

He gets in a huddle with the doctors and I hear the phrase "damage control." They talk about what to tell the parents. The decision is made to meet with each parent or guardian individually to avoid "a mob mentality." They'll hold the meetings somewhere else; getting the news while seeing their unresponsive children would be too upsetting. It's decided that Vesper will stay here and continue monitoring the subjects while Zhu and Osterman confront the parents.

Just before they leave, the beeping of the sensors accelerates like it did before, and they all turn toward the monitors. "What's happening?" asks Osterman, with a note of alarm.

"Eye and heart activity acceleration," responds Zhu. "It's happened before. Brain activity remains flat."

Osterman nods. "Just make sure we keep thorough records of everything that happens." He and Zhu head out the door.

I've been keeping my own records. Jotting down times and events as they happen. Maybe it's because I know so little about the science of sleep disorders, but I've already noticed a pattern, even if they haven't.

I get up and walk over to one of several screens showing the polysomnographic readings. Vesper glances at me. "Is it okay if I look?" I ask.

He studies my face for a moment and decides it's not going to make a difference. "Just don't touch anything."

It's easy to find the place on the graphs where the eye and heart activity jumps. I stand and watch the lines spike up and down for almost one more minute before they plunge and become stable at a much lower level.

The initial plans were to have REM sleep for twenty-minute periods, alternating with fifty-minute NREM phases, both controlled by the electrical current being administered through the electrodes. But even after the electrodes were removed, the feedback from the subjects has risen and fallen in phases close to twenty and fifty minutes.

When Vesper wondered if they could be dreaming, Zhu cut that theory down and said their bodies were just responding to the abrupt interruption in electric flow. But none of them has mentioned the cycles falling into regular intervals. I really don't think they've noticed, which I suppose is normal if they don't think it can have any significance. But could it actually mean something?

I turn my attention to Vesper: his look of intense concentration prevents me from asking. I'm too scared he'll jump all over me for distracting him. I'll wait it out and see if the cycles continue. It's only happened twice. It's probably just a fluke.

I glance over at the seven unconscious bodies hooked up to the Tower and am struck once again with the sensation of being in an eerie science-fiction film. Like the sleepers are pod people, or space travelers held in suspended animation while being transported through galaxies. But these are just kids. They're real people . . . in danger . . . lying a stone's throw away from me.

I glance at the clock and estimate I have another half hour before anything else happens . . . if it happens. I sit back down in my chair, rifle through the folder, and find the section entitled "Trial subject three."

CHAPTER 11

CATA

WHEN I OPEN MY EYES, I AM LYING ON MY BACK on the ground, a wooden floor just inches above my face. I hear yelling and banging and what sounds like a door being smashed in. Boots stomp into the room, and above me the floorboards creak and groan under their weight. Men are yelling in a foreign language, and even though I don't understand the words, I understand the intent: *Come out or be killed.* This is followed by a bout of evil laughter.

I struggle to mask my breathing, but it is difficult not to gasp for air, both from the lack of space and from a wave of panic so severe that it crushes my chest, emptying my lungs. *Breathe in through your nose and out through your mouth* was Dr. Carolan's prescription for panic. I turn my head slightly to the side and pull air through my nostrils, exhaling through my lips as silently as I can. Sweat runs down my forehead, stinging my eyes.

I blink and see Remi lying a few feet away from me, wedged under the floorboards like I am. He works his arm up from his side and places a finger to his lips. As if I need to be told to keep quiet. From the desperate look in his eyes, I know we must be in his story. He knows exactly where we are.

A boot plants hard right above my head. The thin board bows downward under the man's weight and a protruding nail punctures my cheek. I squeeze my eyes shut and grit my teeth against the pain. This is a million times worse than the creepy monster in the cave. I could handle that. It was a monster, not a man. Although sometimes those can be one and the same.

I feel my body numb and my brain start shutting off. *Oh no. It's happening.*

I didn't know it could happen in a dream. I think back to the Flayed Man dream and the cave, and realize that in both of them I was able to do something about my fear: run or fight back. But in real life, when I feel like I'm in danger and can't do anything about it, that's when I'm in trouble. I disassociate. Like I feel myself doing now.

I begin to have the sensation of floating—like my spirit is leaving my body. I hear Dr. Carolan say, *A short break with reality allowed you to escape when the trauma was too intense for you to handle. Dissociation isn't always a bad thing.*

Not when it's going to get me killed, I think, and fight to remain in the here and now. A stream of blood trickles down my face and runs into my ear, the repulsive oozing sensation slamming me back into my body. I resist the urge to reach up and wipe it out. If I move, the men might hear me. I feel it bubble and leak into my inner ear, and I want to scream.

Though the blood half deafens me, I can make out the crashing of furniture and breaking of glass. The boots stop and a second later a spray of bullets riddles down around us, opening up a dozen holes in the floorboards. Light comes streaming through in thin beams. Frozen in fear, my eyes fly to Remi. He hasn't budged.

Seemingly satisfied, the men stamp outside and slam the door behind them. *Are you okay?* I mouth as soon as I'm sure they're gone.

"Yes," he responds almost as quietly. "Just wait."

We lie there, unmoving, until finally I whisper, "Where are we?"

"My home. Crawl space under the floor."

"Why are soldiers crashing around your house?"

"Genocide," he whispers, and that's all I need to know. That explains what he said in the Void—why he left Africa to live with his aunt in America.

I'm in the middle of an African genocide. Or at least a dream about one. A dream so realistic that it almost got us killed. Remi isn't moving. Anguish twists his face, and I wonder if he is rational enough to make a decision for the both of us. "Remi," I whisper. "I want to help you . . . help *us* get out of here, but this is your world, so you need to tell me what to do."

Seeing the suffering in his eyes nudges a memory from my own childhood—something just beyond my reach, but it makes me feel a connection. I watch him steadily, pushing my dread aside. After a second, some of the torment leaves his face, and he blinks a few times. Dust motes and sawdust spin around in the columns of light surrounding us. Finally, he shifts and pushes up a section of attached boards above him. He eases it to one side and pries himself out.

His previous surliness has been replaced by a clinical resolve. It occurs to me that survival is the only thing this boy thinks about. Not making friends. Not being personable. Just survival. And if this is what he comes from, I can see why.

Remi squats down and sticks his face into the hole. "It's safe to come out," he says, and thrusts his hand down to help me crawl out.

We are in a one-room house that has been totally ransacked. But Remi's expression is one of relief: he clutches his chest with his hand and the trace of a single tear remains on his cheek. "They aren't here this time," he says, and, seeing my confusion, explains in a choked voice. "In this dream, sometimes when I come up from below, or walk in the front door, or creep in the back window, my family is here." He gestures at the floor. "Slaughtered." He swipes the tear from his cheek and stands there looking empty.

"Remi," I whisper, "we need to get out of here."

"You're right," he says, and presses his fingers to his forehead like he can force the images away. "Okay. Wait here." He goes to an open window at the back of the room and peers carefully out.

I poke the bottom of my T-shirt into my ear and tip my head sideways, letting it soak up the blood. I inspect the stain on my shirt and run my finger lightly over the blood-matted puncture wound on my face, wincing as I touch the hole. Real blood. Real pain. Does that mean we really could have been killed with the very real-looking bullets that lay scattered on top and beneath the floorboards? What if we never get back to the Void? What if, this time, we're stuck here?

A sound from the street jerks me from my thoughts. *They're coming back,* I think. Fear burns a hole through my stomach. I glance around to see Remi climbing out the window and waving for me to follow him. Lunging across the room, I scramble through the window and follow Remi as he creeps around the side of the house. We hide behind a wooden shed anchored to the house a few feet back from the street. From the smell, I guess it was once used to keep livestock—probably chickens, since there's a little ramp leading up to the elevated door—but it's empty now. I can still hear the sounds of men yelling and shots being fired, but they are coming from farther away.

I wedge myself into the corner behind Remi, who pokes his head gingerly around the edge. I see his body tense, and then he pulls back and turns to me with an astonished expression. "You have to look," he whispers.

I hesitate.

"Don't worry. The militiamen—they've moved on," he reassures me. "Just look at the car to the right of the general store."

I inch forward to peek around the edge of the henhouse. Directly across the street from us is an abandoned wooden building with a few scattered boxes and cans in the windows. Next to it is a rusted-out car with no wheels. And crouched beside the car is the boy from the Void—Ant—dressed in his weird hat and gloves and shorts. He's on his own and looks scared out of his wits. Glancing up, he sees me, and raises a gloved hand to his mouth in surprise.

For a second, it looks like he's going to sprint across the street to us. But before he can, there is a yell and a round of gunfire and the sound of boots coming our way. Remi leans past me to wave the boy back.

The boy's eyes grow wider, and he starts tapping his finger nervously against the rusted metal of the car next to him. It makes a hollow clanging noise. I raise my finger to my lips, but he does it again. *Clang, clang, clang* goes his fingernail against the side of the car.

"Why is he doing that?" I hiss.

"He did that in the cave," Remi whispers. "I don't think he can help it."

"Well, he's going to have to help it or he'll get himself killed!" I lean farther out. A dozen men in uniform are climbing into an army truck parked outside a two-story house on the far side of the general store. One pauses and then turns to walk back toward Ant. I open my eyes wide at the boy, and gesture for him to leave. But he just sits there and folds his fingers together like he's praying and crushes his fists against his chest. He's trying to keep himself from tapping the car, I realize.

Something's wrong with him. He's not going to hide. The soldier is going to find him and kill him.

The gunman has drawn his weapon. Beside me, Remi fumbles in the dirt, picks up an egg-sized stone, and launches it above the army truck. Breathless, I watch it arc through the air over the street. And then it hits one of the house's upper windows with a crash and glass explodes over the truck. The men leap out, firing their guns, pumping the house with round after round of ammunition.

The militiaman near Ant turns and jogs back toward his truck. *It's now or never,* I think, and dashing across the street, I grab Ant's hand. I swoop him up out of his crouch and pull him in a sprint down a dirt path leading away from the main street. Remi is right behind us. "Where do we go?" I yell, and he points toward the outskirts of the village.

We are running at full speed, and I'm practically dragging Ant behind me. "Faster!" I yell.

"I'm trying," he says. His face is white with fear, and I have a feeling that if I weren't pulling him along, he would collapse.

"Do you think they saw us?" I ask Remi, who is pacing me.

"I don't know."

I feel Ant lag and see that he's looking at something behind us. I glance back to see George running to catch up. The others must be here too.

As I try to remember who else was in the Void, I see a movement through the broken window of a house we pass. The door flies open and BethAnn and Fergus burst out, following us at a sprint.

CHAPTER 12

FERGUS

WHEN I OPEN MY EYES, I'M IN THIS RAMSHACKLE building with busted-out windows. It's such a mess, you'd think a tornado had ripped through, except the roof is still there. Outside is a dirt road lined with houses just like this one. There's no sign of anyone . . . anywhere. It's like a ghost town.

I take a minute to get my bearings, wondering if I should hide here or go look for the others, assuming this is like the cave dream and we're all in it together. This place is as hot as hell. A stream of sweat rolls down my back. I fidget, then open the front door and look out. There's no way I'm sitting around and waiting for something to happen.

I wander through abandoned houses for about ten minutes before I find BethAnn. I turn a corner, and there she is—sitting in the back of a dirt-brown army jeep, her hands tied behind her with one of those plastic bands that riot police use as handcuffs. Her face is dirty and her long blond hair is drenched with sweat.

I whistle, and she turns. Her eyes widen with surprise. She shakes her head in warning, and gestures with a tilt of her head toward a nearby house. I nod and hold up both hands, telling her to wait, and then backtrack down the street I came from, ducking into an alley that runs behind the houses. As I near the one she indicated, I hear men yelling in another language and the sound of glass breaking. I approach carefully, staying low to the ground, and see them through a side window: two soldiers pointing guns at a man with his hands in the air.

They're yelling questions at him, and he's answering them and crying. The soldiers' backs are to me, and the man's eyes are glued to them, allowing me to creep toward the street undetected. I scan the room as I pass beneath the window. No one else is there. I move forward, hunched over, until I'm crouching behind the front edge of the house, mere feet away from BethAnn. I whistle again.

Are there only two? I mouth, holding up two fingers, and then pantomime holding a gun. She nods. I inch back a few steps and peer cautiously into the room. The soldiers have forced their captive to sit at a table and have shoved a paper and pen in front of him. One holds his gun to the weeping man's head, while the other stands behind him and shouts.

I dart out to the jeep. "Quick, while they're busy!" I whisper.

Throwing a panicked look toward the house, BethAnn stands and, unable to use her hands, leans toward me. I grab her around the waist and swing her over the back of the jeep onto the street. "This way!" I say, taking her back the way I came. We run silently for a couple of blocks before ducking into one of the houses I already checked out. "There's no one here," I reassure, and pull her through the open front door into a corner where we can't be seen from the street.

BethAnn sinks to the ground. Under the dust and grime, all of the color has drained from her face. I squat down in front of her so we're eye to eye. I tuck her matted hair behind her ear. "Are you okay?" I ask.

She nods mutely.

"Did they hurt you?"

She hesitates, and then shakes her head no. She blinks as sweat drips from her forehead into her eyes. I glance around, looking for a towel or tissues, but the only cloth left in the room is the filthy ripped curtain hanging from the window. "Sorry," I say, and use the bottom of my shirt to wipe her forehead and eyes. She stares at the floor, unmoving.

"Okay, let me find something to get those cuffs off you." I creep over to the front door and ease it most of the way shut, leaving it slightly ajar so it doesn't look suspicious. Then I search a far corner of the room that holds a decrepit sink and rusted stove. I rummage through a drawer under the sink until I find a serrated knife, and saw carefully through the plastic band so I don't cut her.

Hands free, she settles back into the corner, buries her head in her arms, and weeps. I'm not quite sure what to do—I don't have any sisters, and the one girlfriend I've ever had claimed I was useless at comforting. I start to pat her head, but that feels weird, so I sit down and wedge myself in next to her, hesitantly putting my arm around her shaking shoulders. When she seems okay with that, I pull her close.

"It's okay," I say, even though it's not. Who knows if those soldiers will hunt for her house to house, or even if others might burst in and find us?

It's like a hundred degrees, and BethAnn is wearing a long-sleeved white shirt over a tank top and jeans. One of her pink Converse low-tops is untied.

"I'll get us some water," I say finally, peeling my arm from around her. Creeping back to the kitchen, I hold the one unbroken drinking glass up to the tap and turn the spigot. Nothing comes out for a second, and then a trickle of brown sludge streams out. So much for that bright idea.

Returning to BethAnn, I squat down and tie her shoe. "Why don't you take off that shirt?" I ask. "It's like a sauna in here."

She shakes her head. Her damp hair hangs down around her face and the back of her neck is bright red.

"Seriously. You're going to get heatstroke."

She lifts her head, and she is drenched in sweat and tears, her manga-huge eyes bloodshot and puffy. She just stares at me for a moment, searching my face like she's deciding if she can trust me. Then she lifts her hands like a little girl for me to pull off her shirt, and as I do, I see why she kept it on. Her rib cage protrudes sickly through her tank top. But that's not the worst of it. On her wrists, high enough so her long sleeves hid them, are angry red slashes. Pink scar tissue ribbons across them.

She looks me straight in the eyes, daring me to say something. I wait until I can once again speak and then ask, "Why would you . . . ?"

"There was an accident," she whispers. "It was my fault."

"What?" I ask, astounded.

"I don't want to talk about it." Her gaze drops back to the floor.

"Listen . . . I'm sure that whatever happened wasn't worth trying to . . . to . . ." I stammer, not able to say the words. What could be bad enough for someone to want to die?

An image of my father flashes through my mind. My father, who believes I can will my way out of my condition. That my narcolepsy is somehow a choice and if I were just more determined to beat it, I would be "normal." My father, the famous motivational speaker, who inspires crowds with his words, but uses his fists when it's just me.

Okay, I've never wished myself dead, but the thought has crossed my mind that life would be easier without *him* in it. The scene with BethAnn splitting open my monster-dad's skull in the cave replays in my head, and I am flooded with conflicting feelings of guilt and relief.

BethAnn studies my face, and misreads my expression. Her face clouds defensively. "Listen, I'm not suicidal. As soon as I cut my wrists I regretted it and drove myself to the hospital. It was just . . . a really dark time."

"I'm not judging you." I fold her shirt and hand it back to her.

"Whatever happened, it's none of my business. But right now we need to get out of here, so you're going to have to forget everything else and focus."

Her pupils dilate with fear. "I don't want to go back out there."

"Those guys could come back. Or there could be others," I say.

"I don't care. I'm not moving." She wraps her arms tightly around her knees.

Just then, I hear the sound of feet on the dirt road outside. My mouth turns sour with panic before I realize that, whoever it is, they're running in silence. BethAnn's captors were driving a jeep and weren't trying to hide the racket they were making. I go to the window and peer out. Sprinting down the dirt road in our direction are four of the kids from the Void.

"Come on, BethAnn, it's the others!" Not waiting for her reaction, I grab her arm and yank her to her feet.

"Hey!" she yells.

I drag her out the door just as they pass. We fall in behind them. BethAnn jerks her arm away from me and runs on her own.

"There are soldiers down that way," I call to Remi, who seems to be leading the pack. He nods and peels off to the left, zigzagging us down alleys and back lots until we reach a crossroad and he stops. "Hide in there," he says, pointing to a shack made of corrugated metal. It's no bigger than my dad's toolshed. The door has been ripped off and is lying on the ground a few feet away. "I'll be right back," he says before dashing off.

Cata stands there holding Ant's hand. She was dragging him along as we ran. Ducking down, she maneuvers him into the shed, and George and BethAnn and I crowd in behind them. I inhale and am hit with the overpowering stench of manure. Cobwebs hang thick from the corners of the roof, and I step carefully to avoid the dark clumps in the straw strewn across the floor. This must have been some sort of animal pen before it was abandoned. I cover my nose and mouth with my hand like the others are doing, blocking the smell while simultaneously catching my breath from our run.

BethAnn finally breaks the silence. "There are men with guns out there."

"We know," Cata whispers. "We saw them too."

"They took BethAnn captive. I helped her escape," I explain in a low tone. She leans against me, and I wrap an arm around her. "How does Remi know this place?" I ask Cata.

"This is the town he came from. His family was slaughtered here," she responds quietly. "He used the word *genocide*."

BethAnn shivers. I squeeze her tighter.

Something's different about George, but I don't realize what until she adjusts her dress strap. She's changed clothes. Although her Docs are the same, she's lost the tights and is wearing a tan-colored tank dress.

George sees me staring and opens her eyes wide in a silent version of *What?* When I don't respond, she looks away and says, "All of us are here except Sinclair. Has anyone seen him?"

Cata shakes her head. "Remi and I appeared next to each other . . . in his house. We found Ant across the street just before the rest of you showed up."

Ant looks as white as a sheet, like he's about to have a meltdown. Well, that makes two: everyone's scared, but he and BethAnn look like they've passed their breaking point. George puts a comforting hand on his shoulder, drawing him in for a side-hug, and he exhales deeply and looks a little less like his head's going to explode.

A sound comes from outside the shed. Everyone stiffens. Remi plunges through the door, sweating and out of breath. "The main squadron has moved on, but they left teams to comb the houses for survivors. We can't stay here."

"Where can we go?" Cata asks.

"There's a farm outside of the village where we can hide. But to get from the town to the farm we have to cross a stretch of bare desert. We'll be exposed."

"How far's the farm from town?" I ask.

"Two kilometers," responds Remi.

We all stare at him blankly.

"That's one-point-two-four miles," says Ant. Now everyone's staring at him.

George clarifies, "It's like jogging five laps around a track."

That computes. And it's a hell of a long distance to be running out in the open. "What's our other option?" I ask.

"There isn't one," says Remi, looking away from us toward the door. He leans out cautiously, glances around, and says, "Okay, let's go."

"I don't want to go back out there," BethAnn begs, her eyes tearing up again.

I take her by the shoulders and turn her toward me. Conjuring my best I'm-not-taking-any-more-shit-from-you dad-voice, I say, "BethAnn, we have to move. Now."

Somehow that works. She dries her eyes and shakily wipes her hands on her jeans. "Okay," she says, taking a deep breath. "Okay, I'm ready."

Remi books it out of there, and Cata follows, pulling Ant along with her. As soon as we've squeezed out the narrow door, George grabs Ant's other hand, and they take off. I'm careful to stay near BethAnn, but she seems determined now and runs as fast as the rest of us. We reach the last house on the street, and there, standing with his hands in his pockets, looking around like nothing special's going on, is Sinclair.

"Hey!" he calls, looking relieved to see us. "Does anyone know where we are?" His confusion turns to alarm as he registers the fact that we are running for our lives.

"Just follow!" I shout, and he falls in behind us.

The town ends abruptly, and we plunge into the desert: no plants, no trees, just bone-dry red dirt. Remi points to a large building in the distance with a fence around it and a lone tree to one side. "That's where we're going," he calls.

Now that we have a goal in sight, our group picks up speed. This seems doable.

But Ant's pace soon slows, and Cata and George end up practically dragging him between them. The sun is beating down on us with an intensity that seems impossible, and time slows as we struggle through the hostile terrain.

I match my pace to BethAnn's and see that she's crying again. I grab her hand. "You can do it," I urge as we run side by side. "It's not that far."

From beside us, I hear Cata yell, "You have to go faster!" and Ant's small voice yell back, "I can't!"

"Come on, Ant, you can do it," prods George.

"Someone's coming!" Sinclair shouts. I glance back. A jeep is barreling toward us, its tires throwing up clouds of dust. My heart twists with fear. They're going so much faster than us.

And then, from all around, comes a knock so loud it's like a sonic boom. The black wall appears between us and the farm—still a good distance away. It stretches up into the clouds. "Let's go!" I yell as we sprint toward the darkness.

The jeep is gaining on us. I can see the faces of the soldiers—they're the ones who had BethAnn. One drives and the other stands and points a gun at us. We are almost there. The Wall is just yards away.

I hear the crack of a gun and turn to see Ant fall forward, slipping out of Cata and George's grasp. He hits the ground and rolls around holding his leg while blood spurts out of it. The girls try to pull him up, but he's writhing so violently that they can't get a hold on him.

I let go of BethAnn's hand and point to where Remi and Sinclair are disappearing through the Wall. "It's not much farther," I urge. "Run!"

Doubling back, I sprint to where Ant lies. "Hold him still," I yell, and between the three of us, we lift him. Cata attempts to wrap his arms around my neck and George screams, "Stop struggling and hold on!"

Ant immediately goes limp, and I scoop him into my arms. "I've got him!" I yell and the three of us run toward where Beth-Ann waits next to the Wall.

Off to the right, something catches my eye. It's the same weird creature that was in the cave. As before, it flickers like a broken TV, its form barely human. Its features resemble a Picasso portrait: multiple noses, mouths, eyes, all on different planes. Although it's jerking all over the place, it moves quickly in our direction. It reaches toward me, and a static voice grinds out of its gaping mouths—a long, drawn-out "Reeedddd." It lunges for me.

"What the fuck!" I yell, swerving to avoid it. I trip and almost drop Ant before regaining my balance. The second knock comes, shaking the earth and reverberating through my bones.

Cata, George, and BethAnn are waiting near the black wall, their hair and clothes whipping in the wind, watching as I near. "Go!" I yell, and the first two girls turn and approach the darkness. But BethAnn stays, her chalk-white face drawn with fear.

"Just go!" I yell. The gun cracks again, and I hear a bullet whiz past my head. Almost there.

Another shot rings out, and I feel a burning sensation in my right arm. I stumble, dropping Ant, and fall. As I roll on the ground I watch BethAnn's ghostly form walk past me, away from the Wall, struggling against the wind whipping out of it like she's fighting a hurricane.

She turns to me and yells through the howling gale, "My sister was Ant's age when she died. I'm not letting that happen again." She turns back to face the jeep. "Over here!" she yells, and waves her arms wide over her head. The gun cracks multiple times. I watch in horror as her body convulses, riddled with bullets.

No!" I scream, but she falls. Her body lies motionless before a figure darts out of nowhere and begins dragging her by her wrists toward the Wall. It's George. "You get Ant!" she screams as another gunshot blasts and a bullet goes whizzing past my head.

The third knock deafens me, triggering a painful high-pitched buzzing in my ears. Ant is lying still in shock, his eyes glued to BethAnn's bleeding form. I scramble toward him, grab his arm with my good hand, and tug him toward the Wall. Together, the four of us tumble through the black screen into nothingness.

CHAPTER 13

JAIME

TRIAL SUBJECT THREE, BETHANN LINDSTROM, IS nineteen. She suffers from anorexia nervosa and severe depression. In her photo she looks like the poster child for both diagnoses: emaciated and infinitely sad.

From what her file says, she already had "depression and an eating disorder" before something truly horrific happened when she was sixteen. My mouth is dry as I read the story: BethAnn was babysitting her developmentally disabled thirteen-year-old sister when the girl drowned in the family's pool. BethAnn was so crazed with guilt that a week later she slashed her wrists, but came to her senses before she bled out, bandaged herself, and drove herself to the emergency room.

After the incident, she was prescribed sedatives, but once she was weaned off them, she began suffering severe sleep deprivation. The antidepressant she was subsequently given boosted her mood but worsened her insomnia. Her doctor tried her on two different sedating antidepressants, but both caused her to gain weight, and she refused to continue treatment. She was switched back to the initial medication. Her insomnia intensified to the point that she had to drop out of school and was finally recommended for this trial.

Her psychiatrist recommended Zhu and Vesper's experimental treatment, hoping that if the insomnia could be cured, the depression and anorexia might be treated more effectively.

I look at her family history. Raised in Minnesota. Her blond hair, blue eyes, and last name fairly scream of Scandinavian ancestry.

School: Minnehaha Christian Academy. Her psychiatrist noted a moderately religious upbringing by a dentist father and real estate agent mother. Active in church youth group and a handful of local charities.

I see the phrases "excessive guilt and self-blame" and "emotional self-flagellation" and think of how my own problems seem petty compared to what this girl has gone through. I never had someone die on my watch. I can't even imagine how I'd feel if that had happened to me.

My thoughts are interrupted by the low ringing of Vesper's phone. He picks up and begins speaking to Frankel, and I hear him explain the situation once again from the beginning. I look at my clock. Forty-two minutes. If the feedback changes in the next eight or so minutes, it can't be a coincidence. As to what it means . . .

I glance over to where Vesper sits, watching the monitors and reading numbers into the phone. I want to say something. I really do. But I'm too intimidated. If this famous scientist hasn't yet seen a pattern, who am I to point it out to him? There's probably some really obvious explanation that he already knows, and I'll look like a complete fool.

I think of something that Zhu and Vesper were talking about earlier and type "brain waves" into Google. I find a table entitled "Brain Waves: Frequencies and Functions." It lists five different categories of brain waves, organized into two sections: unconscious and conscious. I turn to a new page in my notebook.

Unconscious (brain waves normally recorded during sleep)
Delta (lowest form) = covers most basic instincts
- *Survival*
- *Deep sleep*
- *Coma*

Theta (next to lowest) = emotions
- *Drives*
- *Feelings*
- *Dreams*

Conscious
   Alpha
      • *Awareness of the body*
   Beta
      • *Perception*
      • *Concentration*
      • *Mental activity*
  Gamma
      • *Extreme focus*
      • *Energy*
      • *Ecstasy*

Right after the earthquake, Vesper had said that the sleepers' brain waves were mostly gamma and going off the charts. So they should have actually been conscious at that point—the moment where their limbs all flailed up in the air. Since then he has said a couple of times that the brain waves are mainly delta, which, seeing the subjects' unresponsiveness, is why Zhu declared them comatose. But if they are having some theta waves, as Vesper said, maybe they are dreaming.

In any case, the brain waves aren't changing between the twenty- and fifty-minute periods. It's just the eye movements and heart rates, as well as some of the other things they mentioned, like muscular tension. I'll have to look back and see what else. So if everything except their brain waves suggests they're dreaming, maybe there's something wrong with the brain-wave sensors. Maybe the power outage reset something in the computer.

I check the clock. Forty-nine minutes have passed. I stand and stretch, turning so that I can watch the sleepers in case they transition from one phase to the next. I roll my neck from side to side, and pull my arms across my chest to release the tension in my shoulders. I glance at Vesper, who is hunched over his keyboard, typing, and then back down at the sleepers. For a second, I think I see movement. Was it subject three . . . the girl I was just reading about? I walk to the edge of the platform, and see it again. Subject three whips her head from side to side, as if saying, *No.*

"Dr. Vesper!" I call, just as one of the windows on his screen flashes red. A loud beeping noise comes from the Tower. I can't help myself, I step down the stairs toward subject . . . BethAnn.

"What the hell?" Vesper is on his feet now, leaning in toward the monitor like he can't believe his eyes.

I'm standing next to BethAnn, whose hands have flown up to her chest. She's covering her heart—pressing down on it.

"She's going into cardiac arrest!" Vesper scrambles down the stairs toward me.

"What should I do?" I sound frantic. I *am* frantic.

BethAnn's eyes fly open and fix on my face. "Am I still . . . in Africa? Did Ant make it? The soldiers . . . they shot me . . . it's a genocide . . ." she says, her features frozen in horror as she struggles to get the words out.

As Vesper arrives by my side, the beeping suddenly settles into that horrible sound that signals fatality in every TV or movie hospital scene. The sound of a flatline. Vesper leans over and prods, "BethAnn. Do you hear me?" He spreads her eyelids and presses his ear to her chest, as if he doesn't believe the monitors.

Straightening, he cups one hand over the other and begins doing CPR on the lifeless girl. His oily, dyed-black hair falls over his eyes as he performs the downward thrusts. "Call nine again, Jaime," he says. "Tell them we need a defibrillator down here now!"

I do as he says, then return to his side. "One. Two. Three. Four." The EMTs are there within seconds. I stand to the side, watching in horror as they take Vesper's place, charge the paddles, and begin delivering shocks to the girl's chest. After three attempts, they stop.

"No response," one says.

"Try again," Vesper urges.

They shake their heads. "It's no good. She's gone. She was past saving by the time we got here."

Vesper stares down at the dead girl, his face white with shock.

CHAPTER 14

FERGUS

WE ARE BACK IN THE VOID, AND THIS TIME IT'S already light when we get here. We are all standing in various places in the glaring whiteness, facing different directions. Except for one person: BethAnn. She is lying sprawled on the ground like a broken doll, blood flowing freely from wounds in her chest, arm, and leg.

My hand is still clenched around Ant's wrist from when I tugged him off the sandy ground into the blackness of the Wall. I drop his arm and ask, "Are you okay?" We both stare down at his leg, which is as good as new.

"I'm fine," he says. And then, obviously not fine, he slumps down onto the ground into a cross-legged position. He doubles over, leaning forward at the waist, and wraps his arms over his head. George is right behind us, and with a smooth, feline movement, she slips down beside him, patting his back and rubbing his bony arm. "I'll take care of Ant," she says, "you get BethAnn."

I stand and move toward the bleeding girl, but before I can get to her, something strange begins to happen. She starts fading. All of the color is draining out of her. And then she's gone. Vanished. The floor is a blank space. No blood. No sign that anyone had ever been lying there.

"What . . . what just happened?" Cata is beside me, her eyes wide and wild with fear. Sinclair joins us, and Remi comes running over from farther away. He focuses on the spot we're all staring at and then glances around the group. "Where's the blond girl?"

"She disappeared."

"I . . ." Cata sounds like she's choking. She clears her throat and tries again. "I saw that. I mean, what happened back there? In the nightmare?"

"She got shot," I say. And as I remember what happened, I'm flooded with horror, grief, disbelief . . . they're all scrambled up together. I reach for my tattoo, massaging it with my fingertips, but it's already too late to fight the wave of emotion. I feel the muscles in my neck go slack, and the next thing I know I'm lying on my back with five faces staring worriedly down at me.

"Dude," George says. "What was that?"

I push myself up into a sitting position and press my hand to the back of my throbbing head. My words come out in a slur, as if my brain and tongue aren't connected. "I'm all right. I have this . . . fainting thing. Low blood sugar." I've told that lie so many times I half believe it myself. I put my head between my knees until the wooziness passes.

I rub my eyes and focus on the concerned faces looking at me. "BethAnn saw Ant get shot," I summarize. "When I went back for him, she threw herself between us and the military guys so I could get him to safety."

"She sacrificed herself for you and the kid?" Sinclair asks.

I see the scene like it is happening all over again. The way she threw out her arms, as if to shield us. To offer herself up. "She said something about Ant being the same age as her sister . . . and that she couldn't 'let that happen again.'" I think back to when we were hiding in the shack and BethAnn said something about an accident being her fault. I bet it had to do with her sister. "So yeah, I think she was trying to save Ant."

There is a moment of silence while everyone digests this information.

"I don't get it," Cata says finally. "Ant got shot, but now he's fine. Beth got shot, and she disappeared. Why?"

"This place must be governed by some sort of ground rules," George says.

"Like what?" Sinclair asks. "I mean, besides the obvious back-and-forth between the Void and the nightmares . . ."

George nods. "Nightmares," she says thoughtfully. "That last one was yours, right?" she asks Remi.

He pales and nods. There is no fight left in him, it seems. Or else he's just taking time to recharge.

"Have you had that dream before?" she asks.

"More or less," Remi says quietly. "Sometimes my family is in it. Sometimes I die with them." He chokes on the last words, and presses his forehead as if he can shove his emotions back inside.

"What about the dream before that?" Cata asks. "The cave one?"

I speak up. "That was mine . . . I think. I had vague recollections of being there before, and the monsters kind of reminded me of my dad. Plus, I heard his voice." I'm trying to be flippant about it, but am still horrified by the memory of my father's eyes staring out of the thing's head as BethAnn smashed it with the stalactite.

"Your dad is blue and hairless?" Sinclair asks with a twitch of his lips.

"No," I say, deciding that I don't like his movie-star snobby looks. "All of the monsters had his eyes. It was like he was looking out at me through them."

"That's disgusting," Cata says, and then her eyes widen. "That's why you stopped me from killing that first monster!"

"Oh, man! So we killed your dad in your dream. Multiple times. That sounds pretty Oedipal," says Sinclair.

I scowl. "It's usually *him* trying to kill *me*," I say without thinking and just as quickly shut up. George is watching me curiously, and I don't feel like spilling my life story in front of her.

Why do I care what she thinks?

Because she's just the kind of girl you always go for, I respond. *Artsy, ballsy, supersmart.* Now is not the time for crushes.

Sinclair sees George looking at me, and can't stand sharing the spotlight. "What's up with the costume change?" he asks, leaning in to nudge George teasingly. "I'm totally digging the safari-chic dress. Is this like Adventure Barbie, or something? An outfit for every dream?"

George glares.

"Okay . . . not Adventure Barbie. Slightly Goth band-chick Barbie. With attitude." He dodges as she nudges him back, not at all teasingly. "What? That's a compliment!"

"It's true. You have different clothes," Cata says, giving George the up-and-down. "How did you do that?"

"Who knows?" George says, glancing down and shrugging. She looks back up, scanning the group. "But to get back to the subject, the basic rules here are becoming obvious, aren't they? Like Sinclair put it, we've been traveling between two alternating places: the Void and the nightmares."

"So, Void, nightmares. There are two places inside this . . . place," Cata says, unsatisfied with her choice of words.

"At least, those are the only ones we've seen so far," Sinclair says. "Maybe there are more. Who knows?"

"But from what's happened so far, we know what happens in the nightmares doesn't carry over into the Void. Whether we get messed up, bloody, dirty, injured, whatever, like we did in the cave and the desert back there, we arrive back in the Void untouched."

"Up to a point," I add. "Judging on what happened to Beth-Ann, if you actually get killed in the nightmare, it's game over."

"This isn't a game," said Remi, narrowing his eyes at me.

"It's a figure of speech," I explain.

"So where is she?" Cata asks with a haunted look. "Did her body go back to that place in Africa?"

"Matangwe," Remi fills in. He says it like the word tastes bad in his mouth.

"There's no way to know unless we go back there," Sinclair offers. "And I, for one, hope I never see that place again."

"Maybe she escaped," I say. "Maybe she went back to the real world."

"That's an interesting thought," George says, tipping her head as she thinks it through. "Maybe you can only escape if you die in the nightmare. If you do, your life's your own again."

"Or maybe not," Sinclair says darkly. "Maybe if you die here you die in real life."

"Which is what?" I ask. "What is real life? I still have no clue how I got here. Or where this is. We've already established the fact we are all suffering from memory loss. Remi's the last one to remember anything, and that was . . . when?"

"February fifth," Remi responds.

"So this could be February sixth, or it could be months or even years later. We have no clue. We're all from different places. How did we end up here, together . . . wherever this is?" I run my fingers through my hair and prop my forehead back on my knees, willing my strength to return. Everyone is silent, thinking.

"What if our real bodies are out there somewhere?" I venture, gesturing toward the sky before realizing that there isn't any sky. Just the blank whiteness. "And it's just our consciousness in here, not our real bodies. But we're able to project them into the Void and the nightmares."

George leans down and pinches my bicep. "Does that feel real?" she asks.

"Ow!" I say. "Yes. Point made. Totally real."

"That reminds me of *The Matrix*," Remi says.

"How do *you* know about *The Matrix*?" Sinclair nudges him. "I didn't see any DVD players back in those shacks."

"Oh my God!" Cata says, wheeling around and staring in at him in reproach.

"What?" Sinclair asks, confused.

"Shacks," Cata says.

"Sorry," Sinclair says, holding up his hands in a gesture of innocence. "I don't know the politically correct term for that style of architecture. I'm just saying I'd be surprised if he had access to movies in such a . . . secluded place."

Cata pursed her lips, considering Sinclair's excuse.

Sinclair pats Remi on the arm. "Dude, I'm sorry. No offense," he says, pouring on the charm.

"We had a library," Remi replies, frowning at Sinclair. "Set up by an international aid society. It had a video player and someone donated a lot of movies. It was one of my favorites."

"Okay . . ." Cata says, "Keanu chose when to teleport or whatever into the Matrix. But we have no control over where we go. Whenever the door appears and the knocking starts, we're at its mercy. And once we're in the nightmare, we're stuck there until the black wall appears."

"How about this?" Sinclair says, making his voice low and spooky. "We're stuck in a postapocalyptic *Matrix*-like game where we're just moved between this artificial holding area and our nightmares. It's like we've fallen asleep, but we keep getting sent into dream after dream after dream. Hey, let's call it . . ." And, with a horror-movie flair, he growls, "Dreamfall!"

"Please," I moan, rolling my eyes. "That sounds like a James Bond film."

"No . . . I like it," George says, impervious to Sinclair's sarcasm. "The Real World and the Dreamfall. It might be tipping the scales of ridiculousness, but there's a grain of truth in it. Keep going, Sinclair."

"Okay, so we're under the complete control of the Dreamfall's sadistic gamers, who get their kicks yanking us from one world to the other whenever they want."

"Oh, come on," I say. Sinclair gives me a satisfied smile. He can tell he's getting under my skin, and he seems to be enjoying it.

"We're not completely at the Dreamfall's mercy," George says. "Ant has already started figuring out how it works."

She nudges Ant with her elbow. He looks up from where his head is buried in the arm nest he's made. "Twenty," he says.

Remi rolls his eyes. "What's that supposed to mean?"

George looks at Ant and waits for him to explain. When it's clear he won't, she says, "Okay. When we were in Africa, Ant told me that both times we were in the Void, we stayed for around twenty minutes."

"How do you know?" Remi asks. "You're not wearing a watch,

and I don't see any clocks around." He gestures around the emptiness to prove his point.

Ant holds his fingers to his wrist for a moment. "My resting pulse is eighty beats per minute. I just used it to count the minutes."

"You've been counting the minutes the whole time we've been here?" asks Sinclair with amazement.

"I always count minutes," responds Ant. And then, realizing that we're all gaping at him, he quickly unfolds his arms and taps nervously on the ground four times.

"COULD YOU STOP DOING THAT?!" Remi yells, hands flying to his head like he's going to tear out his hair. *Here we go. The old Remi's back.*

"It's obviously a nervous tic," says Cata. "Just shut up about it. You're the one who said he can't help it." Remi squeezes his temples in frustration.

"I need my notebook and pen," Ant says in a small voice. "I have my hat and my gloves and . . . I have four. I need six. Six is the number. Four is not enough." He taps four times again and looks frightened.

"If we want to get out of here, we shouldn't be taking advice from an autistic obsessive-compulsive timekeeper," Remi says, turning back around and staring at us like he's trying to get us to join his side.

Man, does this place bring out the worst in people. Cata sucks her breath through her teeth, and George's hands curl into fists.

"Like I said before, I'm not autistic," Ant says, straightening his back and speaking forcefully for the first time. He looks Remi straight in the eyes. "I'm not autistic. I don't have Asperger's. I'm not obsessive-compulsive. I'm just . . . me."

Remi looks at his feet, taken aback by Ant's defense.

"Haven't you ever heard of spectrums?" George continues, visibly controlling her rage. "Anyone with half a brain nowadays knows that everything falls on a spectrum. Sexual preference. Neurological normality. Who doesn't have a bit of ADD or dyslexia or addictive personality? And if you don't, I'll bet you've got something else going on."

"So if we've all got problems, what's yours, band chick?" Sinclair quips.

George lifts her chin. "Right now my problem is that I'm surrounded by people who aren't going anywhere except the next nightmare if they continue to waste their time dissing each other."

I rub my tattoo as I feel frustration mounting.

Sinclair spots my gesture. "What's up with your tattoo, anyway, Fergus? Why are you always rubbing it like it's a freaking security blanket?" He grabs my arm and inspects my ink. "What's *DFF* stand for?"

I rip my arm back from him and stick my face about an inch from his. "Right now it stands for 'Don't Fuck with Fergus,'" I growl.

"Holy crap, can we bring the man rage down a level?" Cata says, pushing us apart and stepping between us.

"She's right, I'm sorry," Sinclair says, putting his hands out as if to placate me. "I didn't mean to piss you off. This place is just really getting to me."

He looks sincere, and I feel my tension lessening a fraction. I glance at George. She's looking at me like she expects me to make up and be friends with the asshat. I sigh.

"Yeah, me too. Sorry for jumping on you, but just give me space about the tattoo. It's my own business."

Sinclair nods, not quite looking apologetic, but I'll take it.

George looks satisfied. "Ant, how much longer do we have until the next nightmare?"

"Five minutes," Ant replies without hesitation, and then taps on the floor four times.

"DON'T . . ." Remi begins, but George stamps a brown croc Doc Marten and shoots him a look of pure hatred.

"I think I have an idea about another rule of the Dreamfall," Cata cuts in. "You know how last time the door started knocking, Sinclair ran away from it? He was the last one to leave the Void."

"That was just survival instinct," Sinclair protests.

Cata holds up her hand. "Not judging. Just saying that in the nightmare you ended up really far away from all of us."

Sinclair nods hesitantly as Cata continues. "This time, when we came back from the nightmare, Fergus had Ant by the arm, and they ended up here together."

Everyone just stares at her. "Well, what if this time, before we're sucked through the door, we all stand close to each other? We could even hold hands. Maybe we'll end up in the nightmare together. It might be a safer way to face whatever comes next: as a group."

George crosses her arms, thinking, and Remi looks intrigued, as if finally someone has some semblance of a plan. Even Sinclair seems swayed by Cata's theory. "It wouldn't hurt to try," I say, "although I'm not holding his hand." I nod toward Sinclair, who responds with a laugh.

"I'll hold it," Cata says, and with a whisper of a smile, she reaches out and takes Sinclair by the hand. I reflexively glance at George, in all of her totally hot fearlessness and determination, and position myself next to her.

"Two more minutes," Ant says, rising to his feet. He takes George's hand in one of his, and Remi takes his other. But before we even lock fingers, the first boom sounds. Faint blue lines begin to glow from close by.

By the second knock, the door is clearly outlined in fluorescent blue. The third knock is deafening. As the door swings open, with a groan that sounds like the universe is splitting in two, Ant drops George and Remi's hands and tugs his hat farther down over his ears.

"No!" Cata yells, but it's too late. Our circle is broken as we are swooped up into the air and sucked through the door like dying stars into a black hole.

CHAPTER 15

JAIME

IN MERE MOMENTS, VESPER HAS AGED TEN YEARS. He strides silently to his computer, types in a few words, pulls a page from a printer, and comes back with a clipboard and a pen.

At the top is printed "State Board of Health, Bureau of Vital Statistics, Certificate of Death." He begins to fill out the form space by space, asking the paramedics to double-check absence of pulse, body temperature, and other vital signs. Next to cause of death, he pens something and murmurs, "Do we all concur? Myocardial infarction?"

The paramedics agree, and then sign the document as witnesses. Vesper tells them to leave the body. Zhu will want to see it exactly as it is before it is taken to the hospital morgue. Before the men leave, he asks one to locate Zhu and the director and inform them of the death.

I stand at the girl's side, unable to leave her. At the AIDS clinic, I saw people on the verge of death. I saw dead bodies being taken away. I saw my own father's body, hours after he was shot and killed while on duty.

But I have never experienced the moment of death. Seeing someone there, a person, a living being who looked me in the eyes and spoke to me in her very last seconds. And when that spark that was her humanity—the thing that had made her BethAnn Lindstrom—was all of a sudden extinguished, nothing was left but an empty corpse. It didn't seem possible. One second someone is there, and the next they're just . . . not.

I can't look anymore. I turn and walk back to my workstation. There are still seven windows open on my monitor, but since Vesper cut subject three's video and mic, there are three red lights blinking in the top right corner. I want to click it closed, but am afraid it will mess up the whole system, so I try to ignore it.

I feel Vesper walk up behind me, and I swivel my chair to face him. "I'm sorry," he says. "I don't remember your name."

"It's Jaime," I respond.

He draws up a chair next to mine and looks at me with blood-shot eyes. When I met with them yesterday, he and Zhu fielded a dozen texts and phone calls in the space of a half hour, and said they had back-to-back meetings for the rest of the day. The man probably didn't get much sleep last night, and is now facing what could be the biggest crisis of his career. I can't help feeling for him, even if I don't count enough for him to remember my name.

"Jaime, I know we offered for you to leave before. But I am

going to ask you to stay, at least for a while longer. You were the only person here with me when subject three deceased. You saw it happen. Could you record what you saw? What you experienced?" He nods toward my notebook. "You've been taking notes since we started, right?"

"Yes."

"That's good. I won't ask to see them, and won't suggest what you should include in them, so that I can't be accused of biasing your records in case ..."

In case this goes to court, I think, filling in his blank.

"I understand."

He nods and stands to return to his station.

"Dr. Vesper?" I say, rushing my words before I can chicken out.

He turns. "Yes, Jaime?"

"BethAnn . . . subject three . . . said something to me right before she died."

He lifts an eyebrow, intrigued. "Are you implying that she regained consciousness?"

"Yes. I mean, I think so. She seemed to see me—looked me straight in the eyes—and said something about soldiers with guns."

Vesper's interest disappears. He sighs. "Her brain waves were so low when she expired that anything she said can only be taken as delirious rambling."

"I was just thinking..." I can't believe I'm saying this to a sleep expert, but I feel like I have to ... almost like I owe it to the dead girl. "I was thinking that maybe mentioning soldiers meant that she was dreaming. I mean, when considered along with the occasional spikes in heart rate and muscle tension . . ."

"Sleep is all about the brain, Jaime. The subjects' brain waves have remained primarily in delta. They are in comas, and though no one knows what really happens in a comatose person's brain, the mind is operating at a level that is so basic its only job is to keep their body functions continuing, if even that. What the girl said was like the final spasm of a dying nerve. Thank you for telling me, but please don't worry about it."

He goes back to his desk and sits down, propping his head in his hands for a few moments before sighing deeply and switching on his microphone to begin an oral account of what happened.

I know I should listen to the expert. I know that a premed student can't possibly know more than a man who has dedicated his life to the study of the brain. But I can't help feeling that there is more going on here than what the sensors pick up and spew onto the monitors in beeps and jagged lines. I want to understand what's happening.

I follow Vesper's advice and write down what happened in my notebook, including the parts he said to forget about. I write down the way the girl looked into my eyes. I write down each word she spoke. And then, when I finish, I pick up the test file and flip to trial subject four, Sinclair Jacob Hartford.

CHAPTER 16

CATA

I AM LYING ON MY BACK IN THE DARKNESS. THIS definitely isn't the Void—it is too cold here. My fingers press against something soft and silky. I hear a mechanical *tick, tick, tick,* and a faint green glow comes from somewhere to my left.

I inhale, and my hand flies to my mouth as my throat constricts. Surrounding me is a stench that makes my eyes water. It reminds me of the long-dead dog my sister and I came across in the woods when we were little, but with a good dose of hospital-smelling chemicals thrown in. My stomach sours.

As my eyes adjust to the darkness, the space takes form around me. I am lying under a curtain of some sort. A shiny curtain that is not quite an arm's length from my face. I reach up to touch it, and feel that behind the smooth satin is something hard. Solid. Wood, maybe. I drop my hand back to my side. Beneath me the fabric feels the same, but covers something springy. Cushioned.

I inch my fingers outward, and my left hand grazes something cold and clammy.

I turn my head to see a girl only a foot or so away from me. For a second, I think it's George. She has dark hair with thick bangs swept to one side, as if blown by a gust of wind. Her eyes are closed in sleep. But there's something weird about her. After a second I realize it's that she isn't moving. Even in sleep, there are those tiny movements of the nostrils, the lips, as the sleeper breathes. But this girl is completely still. And then, as I watch, a small beetle crawls out of her nose.

And as horror stabs through me, I realize that the cold, clammy things my fingers are touching are the girl's dead, rotting fingers. I try to scream, but it comes out of my throat as a hysterical screech. As I recoil from her, my right shoulder nudges something soft. I whip my head to the right and am inches away from the decomposing cheek of a boy, rotted away to the point that his teeth are visible through the putrid flesh.

"Oh my God!" My voice is shrill and trembling. Fear crushes my chest so that I can barely breathe.

"Where are we?" comes a voice from somewhere to my left. It's Remi's lilted accent, his words coming out in a squeak.

"We're in a coffin," says Sinclair from my other side. I lift my head slightly to look over the dead boy and see Sinclair lying stretched out like me on the other side of the decomposing corpse. In the faint green glow, I can see another body lying to the right of him. I swing my gaze to my left and see Remi, eyes as big as baseballs, staring my way with a look of pure terror. He's pushed up against the silk on his left at the far end of the coffin.

"Is it just the three of us in here?" I ask.

"Us and three dead people." Sinclair's voice is flat, like he's in shock.

"Who are they?" I ask. "The dead kids."

Neither boy says a word.

"Where are the others?" I insist.

"Ant let go of my hand as we went through the door," Remi responds. "You might have been right about sticking together." He pauses for a minute. "This isn't real, right?"

"It's as real as your *shanty*town," Sinclair responds, "where BethAnn got killed."

Is he trying to bait Remi?

"Or got out," Remi says, not noticing the dig. "She might have actually gotten out of the Dreamfall, remember?"

"What is that noise?" I ask. In this enclosed space, the mechanical ticking is so loud it seems to be coming from inside my head. My heart is beating along with its rhythm. Too fast. Too hard.

"It's a clock," Sinclair says.

"How do you know?"

"It's ticking. What else would it be . . . unless we're in a coffin with a bomb."

I crane my head to the right to see him leaning upward. In the darkness, I can barely make him out, but his lips are curved into a tight smile. "Sorry . . . I have a bad habit of joking at the worst times. Stress relief."

"It's okay," I say, and I want to touch his hand, if only to feel something else warm and living.

"It's an alarm clock," Remi confirms. "It's glowing in the dark. I can just see it if I lift my head. Wait, I'm touching it." And then he squeaks like he just reached out and grabbed a rat. "It's in her hand," he says with a trembling voice.

My brain is starting to function again. It's probably been paused on terror overload and now I'm numb enough to the horror for it to play once more. "We need to see better. Can you take the clock out of her hand and hold it up?"

Another second passes, and there's a scrabbling noise and Remi makes another sound of disgust. "Ugh. Her fingers are locked around it. Wait. Her arm moves."

I pick up my head and try to see what Remi's doing. He's struggling with something over on the other side of the girl. After a second, I see a dead hand ease up over her hip and come to rest on her stomach. Painted fingernails are wrapped around a glittery alarm clock with a round face. The numbers and hands glow neon green. And on the top, where the snooze button should be, sticking out between the girl's dead fingers is perched a plastic figurine—a horse with a tail and mane in rainbow colors.

"My Little Pony?" I squeak. "Why is the dead girl holding a My Little Pony clock?"

"My Little Pony . . . the stuff of nightmares," Sinclair says, with more gallows humor.

"The hands read midnight," Remi comments.

"Is there any way we can stop the ticking? It's driving me

crazy." I reach over to try to wrest the clock from the dead girl's fingers, but she's not giving it up that easily. I accidentally look at her face again, and gag as I see the beetle perch on her lower lip before disappearing into her slightly open mouth.

"Oh my God. I'm going to throw up," I say.

"Might improve the smell in here," Sinclair comments through his fingers. He's holding a hand over his nose and mouth. If possible, the stench seems to be getting worse. Maybe because the three living occupants of the coffin are warming the place up.

Instead of fading into the background like you'd expect, the ticking is getting louder. My brain feels like it's going to explode.

"Are we just going to lie in here, or are we going to try to get out?" Remi says finally. "I can't . . . I can't stand this much longer."

"Plus, if we don't get out before the Wall appears, we could be stuck here," Sinclair adds.

At this horrifying thought, my panic rises and my thoughts begin to cloud. *Don't dissociate.* I try to pull my wits together and focus. I would do Dr. Carolan's breathing exercise, except I'm actually trying not to breathe . . . or at least breathing in short shallow breaths . . . because the stench is so bad.

"Okay," I say, urging my brain into action. "Everything depends on where this coffin is. If we're aboveground, maybe we can get the lid to open."

"We're underground," says Sinclair.

I crane my head to look over at him. "How do you know?" Through my peripheral vision, I spot something moving through the dead boy's gaping cheek, between his teeth. I try to avert my eyes. *It's a millipede,* my brain says. I taste bile, and ignore my nausea. *"Sinclair?* How do you know?"

"Because these people are rotting. They've obviously been dead for a while. You don't just leave dead, rotting people aboveground. We've got to be buried." His gaze falls to the boy between us, and a look of disgust passes over his face.

"Well, since this is a nightmare, who knows? I mean, six people buried in one coffin is already unrealistic. Maybe we're laid out in a viewing room in some creepy *Addams Family*–style mortuary." I try not to think about the last funeral I went to: my mom's. Although we didn't "leave her to rot"—she was cremated within days—Sinclair is right. The boy on my right looks like he's been dead for months, years even.

I reach my hands up to press against the coffin lid. My arms are bent at the elbows—there's not enough space to straighten them. The lid doesn't budge. I try to bend my legs and pull them up to shove with my feet, but there's not enough room. "Let's try to push it open together," I say. "All three at once."

Sinclair presses his palms against the coffin lid, ready to push. Remi is smaller than us, so his arms are already perfectly straight. He tries to replicate my leg movement, and scrunching into a ball, is able to place his tennis-shoed feet against the lid.

"Okay," I say. "One, two . . . push!"

We strain against the lid for a good few seconds, but nothing happens.

"Let's try it again."

"This isn't going to work," Remi responds.

"Doesn't matter. I'm not going to just lie here and hope we somehow get sucked into the Void the next time the Wall comes." I'm disgusted with Remi's defeatism when we've barely even tried.

"Even if we do get out," Remi continues, "what if we're not close enough to the Wall? We had to run for it before. It never just comes to us." He sounds like he's beginning to panic. "What if we're stuck here? Forever?"

"Well, forever's not going to last very long if you hyperventilate and use up all the oxygen," Sinclair responds.

"For God's sake, Remi, just shut up and push." I place my hands back on the lid. "And really try this time instead of giving up before you've even given it any effort."

Remi doesn't deign to respond. He rolls his legs up again and places his soles against the ceiling.

"One, two . . . push!" This time something shifts, ever so slightly.

"The lid," Sinclair says excitedly. "The lid on my end. I think it opened a crack."

"Let's try again!" I urge. We do the same routine about three more times, but nothing else happens, except for the fact that our exertion has made the air a little bit warmer. With it, the horrible dead smell gets worse.

"Well, that was a resounding success," Remi says after a moment.

I ignore him and say to Sinclair, "At least we know the lid

opens on your side. Maybe if all three of us are down at your end and we put more pressure on it, we can get it open a little farther."

"How are we supposed to do that?" Remi asks. "Crawl over the dead kids?"

I paused, not having considered the logistics before suggesting it. "I guess that's the only way," I concede.

"There's barely any room between us," Sinclair says. "How's that going to work?"

I lift my head and check out the space on either side of me. "Remi, try to scoot yourself over the top of the girl. Then we'll try to push her down to the end."

"That means I have to touch her." His voice chokes with revulsion.

"You're touching her already, aren't you?" Sinclair asks.

"I'm trying not to."

"Try to shuffle over her on your back," I suggest. "Don't roll over her front ways or you'll be looking her in the face."

Remi lay there, unmoving.

"Does anyone have a better idea?" I ask. "We'll have to crawl over them at some point anyway. If we manage to open the lid more, we still have to squeeze out of Sinclair's end of the coffin."

I can hear Remi blow loudly through pursed lips, like he's trying to psych himself up. And then there's a scurrying noise as he jams his tennis shoes against the bottom of the casket for leverage while trying to shift his butt and shoulder up on top of the girl.

In a second he's back where he started, lying full-length on his end of the casket. "Her hand's in the way," he says. "The hand with the clock."

"Push it back down beside her," I instruct.

"I can't," he says. "I don't want to touch her again."

"You're about to freaking squish her with your body—what difference does it make if you touch her hand?" says Sinclair, exasperated.

"It's okay," I say. "I'll do it myself, if I can reach." But when I try to push her hand back toward Remi, the clock's thin, pointed legs catch in the knitted fabric of the girl's shroud. I push a little harder, and her hand rebounds and springs forward, tilting the clock face against her chest and extinguishing the little light we had.

Remi sucks in his breath in response to the darkness.

I shuffle to my side and use both hands to try to wedge the clock out of the girl's grasp, pulling on her fingers until I feel one snap. I freeze.

"What was that sound?" Remi asks.

"I-I think . . ." I stammer, ". . . I think I broke her finger."

"Break all her fucking fingers and get the clock away from her so we can see!" Sinclair growls.

I realize with a chill that that's exactly what I have to do. The more I struggle with her corpse, the more her body tightens. There's no other way.

Fighting a fresh wave of revulsion, I get a good grip on the clock with my right hand, and with my left I pull another finger back. It doesn't take much pressure for her brittle bone to snap.

It makes a hollow sound that drowns out the ticking of the clock for one horrific second. I shudder violently and try not to gag. I hear Remi whimper, and then start whispering something. "Hail Mary, full of grace . . ." He's praying in the darkness.

Yeah, well, I don't have a god to pray to. Not anymore. But I have my cabin in the woods.

It's my safe place. The one Dr. C had me create. I've never actually laid eyes on more than an inch of snow in my life, but this is what popped into my mind when he told me to think of somewhere safe.

I'm inside a cozy one-room cabin hidden in the snowy woods. I'm stretched out on a couch, wrapped up in furs, and there's a roaring fire in a fireplace. The snow outside the windows is thick, and there is no visible path leading to civilization. No one can get to me. I feel my heart slow from a fast, painful thump to a slow regular beat. The fire crackles and warms my skin. I feel my breathing shift from panicked to even.

As I feel the horror rise inside me, I shove it back down with thoughts of the crackling fire and soft furs. I try to focus on the white snow outside the windows instead of the fact that my lungs are absorbing airborne molecules of decaying children. I take a third finger and pull it back with all my force, ignoring the snap and going immediately for another.

And then I'm holding the clock and can see again. The girl's mouth has fallen wide open. It looks like she's silently screaming. As I'm seized by a blinding white fear, I feel something happen in my head. Like my brain is disconnecting and my body getting lighter, and I realize that if I don't focus I'm going to dissociate. There's a difference in thinking about the cabin in the woods in order to calm down and actually going there. And although it would be the nicest thing in the world to let my brain escape what my body cannot, I remind myself that *this is not the time.*

I breathe in deeply, and the putrid air brings me back to myself in an instant. "Hold this," I say, shoving the clock at Sinclair. He sets it on his chest, facing me, illuminating the space with its glowing green aura.

I turn and, reaching over the girl, wrench her arm back down to her left side. "Now!" I say to Remi, and he swings his feet up above the girl's and pushes them against the bottom of the casket as he wriggles his way up on top of her. His body is wedged between hers and the casket lid. "Keep going until you're on the other side of me," I say. As soon as he lifts himself off her, I begin shoving the girl sideways with my shoulder and hip, fitting her into the space Remi just vacated. As he shuffles over me, his elbow jabs me hard in my gut, and I gasp for air.

"Sorry!" he says.

"Just go," I pant, and use all my weight to shove left. I don't even look at what I'm doing to the body beside me, I just free up as much room as I can until Remi tumbles into the space I've made on my right.

We both lie there panting. Now that I'm done with the girl, I try to pretend she's not there. That there's nothing to my left . . . just empty casket.

"Well, that's one down. Two to go," Sinclair comments darkly.

"Your turn to do some of the work," I huff. "Remi, do the same thing as before. Crawl first over the dead boy to your right and then over Sinclair. While you do, Sinclair will push the dead boy toward me."

"Why do I have to move?" Sinclair asks. "Can't Remi push the kid over by himself?"

"The girl was heavy," I reply. "Remi's like half your size. You and I can do the grunt work." Sinclair mumbles, but shifts his feet and arms in preparation.

Remi gets into position, reaches over the boy to begin shuffling backward over him, and freezes. "What's this?" he asks. "This was lying on his stomach!" In the shallow space above us, he grasps a hunting knife in his fingers. The green clock light glows off the sinister blade.

A gasp of surprise escapes Sinclair's lips.

"What's wrong, Sinclair?" I ask.

"First a My Little Pony clock and now a slasher-film bowie knife?" he says, recovering his cool a little too late. His reaction to the knife seemed excessive compared to how he's been handling the rest of this gory scene. A little seed of doubt plants itself inside my mind . . . Could this dream be his, and he's pretending he hasn't seen it before?

"This has got to be the weirdest dream in the history of nightmares," he explained. "I wonder what this one's got." There's a sound of scuffling. I lift my head to see him patting down the corpse on the far end of the coffin. There is a jingling noise, and he holds something up for us to see. "Keys. This one's holding keys."

"What does it mean?" Remi asks.

"We don't have time to think about it," I say. "Sinclair, push the one on your right up onto its side and against the end of the coffin. That gives us a few more inches of space. Remi, give him the knife to set on top of the end corpse. We might be able to use it to wedge the coffin open farther. Keep the keys, Sinclair. Who knows what they're for."

I hear the keys clink as Sinclair shoves them into his pocket, and then the shuffling sound of him shoving the last corpse as far over as he can.

"Okay, Remi. Go. Get over Sinclair, and wedge yourself next to the last corpse," I say. There are a claustrophobic few minutes or so of grunting and shoving before everyone is in place.

"Done," Remi says.

"Okay, Sinclair," I say. "I'm going to crawl on top of this boy and over you. Once I'm on top of you, try to shove him over next to the dead girl, and I'll roll into place between you and Remi. Ready?"

Sinclair looks uncertain, but nods. I take in a lungful of toxic air, and, holding it in, inch my feet to the top of the coffin and try to shift my body backward up on top of the boy. I know immediately that it's not going to work. My butt is wedged against the boy's hips and my hands are trapped on either side of him. I quickly shift back into my previous space.

"I'm going to try it on my front." I say the words trying not to think about what they mean.

Summoning all of my strength, I roll up onto my side and then forward up onto the boy, reaching over him to grab Sinclair's hand. Sinclair pulls my arm as I shuffle over the body. My knees knock hard against the leg bones as I arch myself up, trying not to touch anything else.

Sinclair pries one hand between me and the boy and, grabbing me by the waist, attempts to pull me onto him. I squeeze my eyes shut as my head passes over the dead boy's face, scrambling with superhuman strength over the putrid corpse. But I open them too soon, and instead of looking at Sinclair, I am staring into the dead boy's empty eye sockets. Which are teeming with maggots.

I can't help myself. I'm no longer in control. I scream, loud and long, flailing as I try to get away, and my panicked movements pitch me forward, flat onto the boy. For one claustrophobic moment, I am stuck. My cheek is wedged against the dead boy's rotting flesh, which squishes wetly next to my ear. I want to scream, but feel something slither against the edge of my mouth, and press my lips tightly shut.

My heart stops. My brain turns off. I feel my body being pulled onto Sinclair, who is shoving the boy corpse away from us with all his might. With a roar, he gives the body one last shove. Remi's hands tug at the back of my shirt, rolling me limply into the space between him and Sinclair, as Sinclair shuffles far enough to his left for me to land on the cushioned base of the coffin.

"Are you okay?" Remi asks me.

But my lips won't move. My eyes stare blindly at the top of the coffin as the form of a man begins to materialize against the purple silk. In slow motion, he folds a leather razor belt in two between his hands, and then snaps it loudly.

"We'll have to push without her." Sinclair's words barely register in my mind as my father's shape looms over me. "One, two . . . push!" I hear from worlds away, and then they've disappeared and I'm alone with my dad.

He snaps the belt one more time, and then lets go of one end and rears back with one arm. "I'm going to break that stubborn will of yours, Catalina. And this time, I'm not stopping until I see you cry."

CHAPTER 17

FERGUS

I AM SITTING IN THE CORNER OF A ROOM, LOOK-ing at five long rectangles of light shining through the wall in front of me. Against my back is cold, hard stone. I wrap my arms around my knees for warmth. This place is freezing.

As my eyes adjust to the darkness, the light columns transform into a window divided by vertical iron bars. Outside, I see dead tree branches and the sliver of a moon. Between me and the window is a large hunk of stone . . . what looks like an enormous gray box, so old it's crumbling at the edges.

The place smells musty, and thick cobwebs stretch like translucent curtains from the corners of the ceilings to the leaf-strewn floor below. *It looks like an over-the-top set for a low-budget vampire movie,* I think as I scramble to my feet. The little square room is a mausoleum, and the box in the middle is an enormous granite tomb that takes up most of the space.

"Fergus!" I hear George's voice and look over to see her huddled with Ant in the far corner. Ant's head is down on his knees, two fingers on one wrist—taking his pulse, I suppose—and George has her arm around him.

I scoot past the sarcophagus toward them, pausing to take a long glance out the window. "Are you guys okay? Where are the others?"

Without looking up, Ant says mournfully, "I let go of Remi." He taps the ground four times, and then wraps his arms around his knees and peers out at me from beneath the knit chullo with wide, scared eyes.

"Where are we?" George asks.

"In a graveyard. Or, more specifically, in a mausoleum in a graveyard." I offer her my hand to help her up.

She looks at it for a second, like she's considering whether or not to accept my help. Her eyes flick up to mine, narrow, and she tilts her head to one side. I have never felt so analyzed . . . so judged . . . in my life. But apparently I pass muster, because she sighs and, grabbing my hand firmly in hers, drags herself up, bringing Ant with her.

"What's outside?" she asks, brushing dead leaves off her legs. She's wearing the same punk-looking plaid miniskirt and black band T-shirt she was the first time I saw her, but something's different. I can't quite place a finger on it, but don't want to stare and risk drawing her wrath.

"Creepy old trees. Moonlight. Crumbling graves. You know,

the usual." I try to sound flippant. Brave. "Looks like a mash-up of *Carrie* and *Return of the Living Dead* with a touch of *Pet Sematary*."

"Wow, sounds like you really know your classic horror films," George says.

"Yeah, I've seen pretty much every one ever made. Multiple times," I admit.

"I don't like scary movies," Ant says, watching me with mistrust.

"I never said I liked them."

George laughs. "You are a strange boy, Fergus . . . whoever you are."

"Tights," I respond.

"Fergus Tights?" George says, arching an eyebrow.

"No, your tights. They were like a neon yellow before. Now they're purple."

She looks down at her legs, at Ant, then back at me, and shrugs. "Well, purple is my favorite color. And, by the way . . . someone's tights are probably not the first thing I would notice if I found myself standing next to a sarcophagus."

She presses her lips together in a teasing smile, her eyes sparkling with repressed humor. The way she said it—the way she says everything, with that bone-dry humor—makes me want to laugh.

Oh no, not again. I repress it . . . twist the funny out of it as I press hard on my tattoo. I clear my throat and the feeling of hilarity is fortunately gone.

George loses her smile and looks curiously at my arm. "I know you didn't want to tell Sinclair about it. But I'm curious . . . what's with the ink?"

I shrug, not wanting to get into it. "What's with yours?" I ask, looking at the minimalist yin-yang tattoo on her wrist.

"Symbolic," she says mysteriously. "Someone else chose it for me."

A boyfriend, I think. *Of course she has a boyfriend. How could she not?* "Let's get out of here and find the others," I say.

The barred window is set in the upper half of an ancient iron door. Its glass, presumably meant to keep out the elements, has failed at its mission, and is letting in a stream of cold night air through a broken section in the top right corner. I try the creaking doorknob, twisting it carefully back and forth before putting more muscle into it. "It's jammed," I conclude.

"Or locked," George suggests. She clears away the cobwebs inside the door frame and presses her head into the corner of the lintel to peer sideways out the window. "There's a key in the lock outside." She looks down at her hand, and then at Ant's. "Ant's arm is small enough to fit through the bars if we can break the glass near the doorknob."

My hands automatically go to my pockets to see if I've got anything we can use, but they're empty.

George watches me with that intense stare of hers. She's giving me a kind of sideways smile. The kind my old girlfriend used to give me before making some comment like *Oh, Fergus, you're so adorable.* Which she never actually meant as a compliment. It was more to say, *You're a bumbling idiot but I like you anyway.* I feel my face redden.

George's smile widens a fraction, but she has mercy and sweeps her gaze away from me and across the room. "God, this place is empty. The Dreamfall doesn't exactly equip one for surviving its nightmares."

"No," I agree. I run my hand through my hair and peer around the space. "Not much here to break glass with."

"How about this?" George moves to the head of the sarcophagus, which is crowned with a marble cross the size of one of my dad's prized golfing trophies. She pulls on it with both hands, but it doesn't budge.

"You can't break that off!" I say, surprising myself by the dismay in my voice.

"Why not?" she asks. "Are you religious or something?"

"No. I mean, my mom's Hindu. But it's got to be really bad karma to . . . what . . . defile a religious object?"

"The cross is a man-made symbol of a concept representing security in the afterlife for one of several rival world religions," George says. "If a god exists out there, I don't think she'll mind." And backing up, she performs this perfect jujitsu swing kick, her Doc Marten breaking the cross cleanly off at its stem and toppling it to the floor.

My jaw drops. I stare in a mixture of disbelief and awe.

She smiles at me, bemused. "You're catching flies," she comments, tapping my chin lightly with her finger, before bending over to scoop up the granite cross.

Within minutes, we've broken the glass out of the entire left section of the window. I've cleaned the splinters away from the sill with the bunched-up edge of my T-shirt, so Ant won't cut himself. He easily sticks his hand through and pulls the key out of the lock and back through the window.

With a bit of effort, it turns in the lock, and we are outside, standing on a hill overlooking a graveyard that stretches so far in every direction that we can't see an end to the jumbled, misaligned rows of stones. Besides the swaying of the dead clawlike branches of centuries-old trees blown by bone-chilling gusts of wind, nothing moves among the graves. Although the moon shines large and cold, it isn't dark yet. Just gray and dismal-looking, like it's going to rain, but there are no clouds in the sky.

"Where do you think the others are?" I ask, raising my voice to be heard above the wind, which picks up and begins to howl.

"How far apart have we been when we landed in the nightmares the last couple of times?" George asks. Her hair whips around her face, and she brushes it out of her mouth.

"In the Cave, we were one room over from you. Not far," I say.

"In Remi's village, Sinclair was the farthest, and that was about eight of those village blocks away," George reflects.

"They can't be that far, since we were standing pretty close in the Void before Ant let go." He flinches at my words and frowns at me. "Hey, it's okay. You didn't mean to," I add. He just looks down at his shoes.

"There are three paths leading down the hill. Why don't we split up and each take a path to see if we spot anything?" I suggest.

"Out of the question," Ant says, looking terrified.

George glances at him, and then lifts her eyebrows at me as if apologizing. "How about Ant and I go together? You can take another path. It's probably wise to keep in view of each other."

I don't feel like arguing with a terrified thirteen-year-old. "Okay," I agree.

George reaches out and squeezes my hand, looking at me gratefully with her Cleopatra eyes, and my heart does this little stuttering thing. I feel like face-palming. *Sad, Fergus. You are a sad, sad human being.* I turn away from her to walk down one of the paths, alone with my shame.

But I quickly realize I should have been paying more attention when I chose the direction I took. My path's definitely the spookiest. Its uneven dirt is lined with wild, untrimmed trees extending long, fingerlike branches. The stones are mostly crumbling, besides a few newer ones scattered here and there.

I glance over at Ant and George. They're holding hands, walking down a paved walkway leading to a more recent, well-tended part of the cemetery. I turn my attention back to the decrepit plots around me as I make my way down the path, scanning the area for anything out of the ordinary.

There's not much to see, besides a ramshackle shed halfway down the hill. I make my way toward it, glancing down every few feet so I won't stumble over the tree roots poking up through the earth like booby traps on either side of the trail.

The shed is made from the same big blocks of yellowing stone as the mausoleum at the top of the hill, but is small and square with a flat roof. I assume that it's not the right shape for a sar-cophagus, and when I peer through the broken window, I see I'm right. The tiny space is lined with tools: picks, shovels, and gardening utensils. An old-fashioned push lawn mower with a horizontal helix of metal blades stands rusting in one corner.

I hear a loud caw, and jump back from the window. A raven perches atop the roof, staring at me in that way that only the avi-ary spawn of Satan can. I hate ravens. They freak me out. But this one looks like he's about to open his beak and speak, and we *are* in this weird nightmare, so I stare right back at him and wait. "Got anything for me?" I ask him finally. "Some kind of wisdom to impart? A message from the others?"

The bird cocks his head and looks at me like he thinks I'm insane.

"Who are you talking to?" comes a voice from behind me, and my heart leaps into my throat before I turn and see it's Ant, peer-ing at me suspiciously.

"No one," I say, and jam my fists into my pockets.

"You were talking to the bird," Ant says. "I saw you." He looks nervously up at the raven, who eyes us before cawing loudly and flapping off to perch in the top of a tree.

"George thinks we've found something," Ant continues, and begins walking off among the graves, stepping carefully over fallen branches, before looking back to make sure I'm following. We make our way toward the newer part of the cemetery, where George stands staring at something.

She points to a tombstone. "Weird, huh?" she says.

The stone is made up of three separate slabs placed one next to the other so tightly that there's barely a crack in between. They're each carved with different styles of writing but contain basically the same information. Name. Birth and death dates. And a couple of lines from a poem beneath.

"All three of them died in the last couple of years," George remarks.

I do the math. "One was fourteen. The other two, sixteen."

"Three teenage deaths on three different dates, with three different last names. So why are they all bunched here together?" George muses.

"They all have the same poem," Ant points out, and begins reading.

"The traitor spread honey atop pretty lies.
Only the love of his victims he asked.
For deceiving the lamb is the wolf's cherished prize.
And only in death is the true beast unmasked."

"That sounds more like one of those cautionary fairy tales that were supposed to scare kids into being good," I comment, bracing myself against a gust of wind that is so strong it almost blows me over. The cold filters through my vintage *Night of the Living Dead* T-shirt. Although I was dressed perfectly for the African dream, I am pitifully underdressed for a cold windy night in a graveyard. I feel oddly jealous of Ant's weird but warm-looking woolen hat and gloves. I wish I had come better prepared. As if you could pack for nightmares.

George casts a sweeping glance across the graves around us. "Well, this is the only thing that looked out of place to us, if we're not going to go too far from where we landed. Did you find any..."

Before she can finish her question, the ground below us thumps. As if someone pounded on a drum, just once, deep beneath our feet.

"What the..." George says. We stare at the ground. She looks up at me, white-faced. "What do you think that was?"

Although it's cold, the palms of my hands are sweating like they've sprung a leak. "We're in a nightmare," I respond. "It could be anything."

"It came from directly under us," states Ant. "From the grave."

We all stand still, listening until George gets down on the ground and presses her ear to the earth. "I hear something," she says after a moment. "There's something down there, scrabbling around."

"Some*one* down there," Ant corrects her. George raises herself up to her knees and the two look at each other, a look of mutual terror passing between them.

"Could it be them?" I ask. "Could it be Cata and..." I blank on the others' names before remembering. "... Remi and Sinclair?"

"It could be the bodies of those three dead kids on the tombstones coming back to life," George says, losing what was left of her cool and looking flat-out scared. "We could be in a zombie nightmare."

And then the sound of a shriek comes from below us. A shriek that lengthens and deepens into a scream worse than any I've ever heard in a slasher film. A scream of pure, unadulterated horror.

"It's Cata," says George. "She's buried alive. We've got to get her out."

"How?" My thoughts flounder a minute before I remember the toolshed. "Shovels," I say. "I saw picks and shovels in a shed just over there."

I start running, and George is on her feet in an instant, following me. "Stay there," I yell back to Ant.

"Yeah, right!" he yelps, and barrels after us.

In mere minutes, we've broken into the shed and are dashing back toward the triple grave, each toting a pick and shovel. I attempt to shovel into the hardened ground and quickly revert to the pick, axing it through the dry, dusty earth like I'm possessed by a whole mosh pit full of demons. The three of us are digging for all we're worth, breaking the soil with the picks and then shoveling it away. Breaking and shoveling. In no time, sweat is pouring down my face, and the flying dirt coats my skin.

Voices begin to arise from the ground beneath us—male voices this time—and I can make out Remi's African accent as well as Sinclair's lower, rougher tone. "Help!" "Get us out!" they yell, and we are digging a mile a minute, standing hip-deep in earth, when I happen to glance up and see something floating across the tops of the graves toward us.

It's the weird static creature that's shown up in the last two nightmares. It flickers in and out, its multiple mouths grimacing, dead eyes bulging, as it jerks and flashes its way toward us.

"It's the monster thing!" I yell, and George and Ant stop their digging and look in the direction I'm pointing.

Ant's eyes grow wide. "It showed up right before the Wall appeared both times. What if . . ." He stops talking and begins digging even more feverishly than before.

"What if what?" I yell. The monster's getting closer.

George looks up at me, a wild look in her eye, and answers for Ant—almost as if she's reading his mind. "If the Wall comes, we'll be able to escape into the Void. But we'll be leaving the others here, buried underground!"

"Shit," I say, and, tracking the monster's approach in my peripheral vision, attack the earth with renewed frenzy. Two more strokes, and my pick hits something hard. "I've got it," I say. George and Ant come over and help me.

A voice that sounds like beads of water sizzling on a hot iron hisses, "Reeeeedddddddd."

I look up and the monster is standing-floating-standing on the ground beside us, its head leaning slowly to one side and eyes widening horrifically as it watches us. This time it's shape-shifting from what looks like a squidlike alien thing with tentacles instead of arms to human and back again. It takes a step in Ant's direction, grasping at him with a long, rubbery appendage.

Ant shrieks and swings his shovel at the thing, its blade passing smoothly through the static like a hot knife through butter. The fingers-tentacles-fingers keep reaching, inching forward as the thing opens its multiple mouths and moans, "Red."

It brushes against a shovel lying at the edge of our pit, and the shovel sticks to its arm like a weak magnet, bobbing as it levitates slowly into the air. Ant is now up to his shoulders in our grave pit, and the shovel swings dangerously close to his head.

George screams, "Don't even think about it!" and, lifting her pick in both hands, throws herself at the thing. I expect the pick to slice through thin air like Ant's shovel did, and I dodge out of the way. Instead, the improvised weapon hits something and drags, tearing through what might be the monster's side if it didn't keep flashing in and out. The night air is pierced by a scream like nothing I've ever heard: as if God scraped giant fingernails down a galaxy-sized chalkboard.

George drops the pick and clasps her hands over her ears, as do Ant and I. The monster thing staggers backward, jerking grotesquely as it moves away from us.

Its out-of-control flailing transports me back to something I saw years ago. Mom was driving me home from a movie and our headlights caught something ahead on the road, violently bucking up and down. It looked like an invisible hand was repeatedly jerking it up a foot into the air and then smashing it back down onto the road. It flopped around like a fish on dry land, but going way too fast. And then I saw the cat's long tail and bloody fur.

"Oh my God," my mom shrieked, swerving to miss it. I whipped my head around to watch it flip spastically in our taillights.

"We have to go back and save it!" I yelled, my throat dry with horror.

"It's already dead, Fergus." My mom was holding her hand to her chest as if to stop her heart from falling out.

"Then why is it still moving?" I asked, a tear running down my eight-year-old cheek.

"It was killed by another car before we got there," she explained. "Now it's just the nerves reacting."

The way the monster is wildly spasming reminds me of the dying cat.

I'm jerked back to reality by the realization that it was trying to kill us. I swallow my nausea and scoop my pick back off the ground to continue the fight, but the thing has receded into the distance, behind a group of trees.

"Dig!" I urge, and the others grab their tools from the ground.

George's pick is dripping with blood. "Ugh," she yells. She throws it back down, and scoops up her shovel from where the monster dropped it.

We've cleared away what seems like a huge area of earth, but the outline of the box beneath us just keeps on going. The thing is enormous. After a few more minutes of frenzied digging, we have cleared the edges of a massive coffin. Big enough for six people, I think, shuddering as I realize what this means. Surely they're not down there with the dead teenagers. George meets my eyes, and I can tell she's thinking the same thing.

All of a sudden, from the sky, comes a boom like a cannon shot. "Oh my God!" George yells, and dropping her shovel, she grabs the bloody pick and uses it to carve out the ground around the outline of the coffin. Apparently, the boom was heard underground as well, because renewed sounds of yelling and banging come from beneath our feet.

"No time to dig it all the way out," I yell. "Let's just try to pry the lid open far enough for them to escape!"

"We're almost there!" George yells to them.

There's silence from underground, and then . . . *thump* . . . like we had heard before, but much clearer now.

Ant's eyes are popping out of his head in fear, but he stands still, pick in hand, watching the ground. "There!" he says, pointing to one side of our excavation. "The ground moved there when they banged on the lid."

There is a thin seam in the dirt along one edge of the coffin. George and I scramble over to it, and wedge a shovel and pick beneath the lip of wood. We press all of our weight on our tools, trying to jimmy the lid open. There's only enough room for the two of us. Ant crawls out of the pit, and stands to one side, holding his gloved hands to his cheeks and looking like he's about to faint.

There is another boom from the heavens, and the black wall materializes a ways away, between us and the old section of the graveyard. "Faster!" Ant screeches. George and I strain at our tools, and the earth gives slightly, dirt falling away from a shiny mahogany edge as the lid comes up an inch. There is another thump from inside the coffin, and the lid eases open a few more inches, causing our tools to disengage and George and I to tumble against the earthen side of our pit.

Thump. With a jerk, the lid leaps up, leaving about a two-foot opening. A thin, dark-skinned arm reaches through it, tosses aside a knife with a broken blade that had been used to pry the lid open, and scrabbles at the side of the coffin like it's trying to claw its way out. George and I lunge forward and force the lid open another few feet. A fog of toxic-smelling air releases around us, causing me to double over, gagging. George grabs Remi's outstretched arm, and with what seems like superhuman strength, heaves him up out of the box. Ant reaches down from the edge of the pit to take Remi from George and pull him up to ground level.

George yells, "Run!" and points toward the black wall. The boys hesitate for a second, watching us guiltily. "Just go!" I yell. "Get a head start!" And they're off, scrambling through the gravestones at top speed.

Cata lies in the coffin, eyes open but unmoving as Sinclair reaches up and grabs George's outstretched hand and starts scrambling out of the box. Two corpses are wedged into either end of the coffin, upturned on their sides as if hiding their faces against the purple cushioned walls. Another corpse, face caved in and teeth bared in a skeleton's grimace, lies next to Sinclair. As he scrambles to get out, he steps on it, crushing its ribs with a sickening crunch.

"Is she dead?" George asks, her voice rising in hysteria as she focuses on Cata's unmoving form.

"No," responds Sinclair. "I think she's in shock."

"Grab her hand," I say. Sinclair and I crouch down and, taking Cata's hands, pull her limp form up and out of the casket. Her head drops back and her mouth falls open.

"Cata! Wake up!" George slaps her face very gently, but with no effect.

"We have to get her out of here!" I say.

George and Sinclair scramble up to the grassy edge of the pit, and reach down to pull Cata up to ground level. By the time I climb out of the pit, she's able to hold her head up.

As the third boom comes and the wind rises, I squat down next to her and stare into her blank eyes. "Cata!" I yell over the howling gusts. Her eyes roll to the side and then focus on me. "We have to run," I urge. "The Wall's about to close!"

I drape one of her arms around my neck and yell, "Sinclair, get the other side!" The two of us yank her off the ground, and to her feet.

Her lips move, and I lean in to hear what she says. "Can't . . . walk. Legs won't work."

"How about your arms?" I ask.

She squeezes weakly with the arm that's around my neck. "Okay, then hold on to us the best you can," I say. "Sinclair! Four-handed seat!"

"What?" he asks, confused.

"We link our hands and she sits on our arms."

Sinclair throws a worried glance at the Wall as we scoop Cata up in our arms. She manages to hang on loosely to our necks. "Let's go!" I yell, and we take off, George running ahead, steering us through the gravestones and around fallen branches.

We're on the last stretch, running full speed at the Wall, when out of nowhere the monster reappears, jerking and flashing. As George runs past it, it reaches out and claws at her. She shrieks and bats it away, but it clings to her, stopping her from going through the Wall, its horrible, scraping scream barely audible over the roar of the wind.

I veer in her direction and, sensing what I'm doing, Sinclair works with me, running with Cata straight toward George's flailing form. We hit her with all our force, diving hard into her, and sweep her off her feet and into the darkness.

CHAPTER 18

JAIME

TRIAL SUBJECT FOUR, SINCLAIR HARTFORD, SEVEN-
teen, lives on the Upper East Side of New York City with his
ob-gyn father and work-from-home mother. He's a senior at one
of Manhattan's most prestigious private high schools, and his
therapist is one even I've heard of: she's always on CNN giving
her opinion on mental-health-related news stories.

Sinclair's summary is brief: chronic insomnia that affects
his schoolwork and extracurricular activities (tennis, boating,
lacrosse). There is a list of pharmaceuticals that he has tried, but
all have had negative side effects. There is even one account of
him taking Ambien, and then commandeering a waiting taxi
and driving across town without knowing what he was doing.

He has been in therapy since a young age, but all files from the
last five years are sealed by a court order. There's a police file, but

only the barest of details are listed: underage gambling, book-making, blank checks, and other things that don't seem very exceptional for a superrich kid. The footnote, "Additional files accessible by warrant only through the NYPD," mystifies me.

What could this privileged white boy have gotten mixed up in that would call for sealed records? Could whatever it is be a clue to the source of his insomnia? He doesn't have narcolepsy or PTSD or depression like the other subjects I've read about. There isn't a good explanation of what is stopping him from sleeping. Maybe the missing court file contains more information on his mental health.

I look up from the file and Google his parents. Hundreds of pages about charity work, museum sponsorships, and club memberships pop up. There are photos of Sinclair and his parents posing in formal clothes, arms draped casually around politicians and celebrities, champagne glasses raised.

I take a look at the subject four window on my screen, and there he is, looking similar enough to the rich kid in the photos to recognize. But in a hospital gown, and with sensors attached all over his body, he could be the poster boy for *Money doesn't buy happiness.*

Zhu and Osterman burst into the lab. "What the hell happened?" Zhu cries.

With a pained expression, Vesper responds. "Subject three went into cardiac arrest, no warning."

"Did any of the others show signs of cardiac stress?" Zhu asks.

Vesper shakes his head.

Osterman combs his fingers through his nonexistent hair. "For fuck's sake, this is all we need right now. And a minor as well."

"She was nineteen," Vesper mumbles.

"Well, thank fuck for that!" the director roars.

Zhu steps down into the testing area and walks over to Beth-Ann. As she checks the sensors, she detaches them one by one, peeling off the electrodes and pulling out the IVs until the girl is just a body lying on a bed in a white hospital gown. She looks more pitifully fragile than before.

Zhu tests everything manually, feeling the girl's pulse on her throat and her wrist and pressing her ear to her chest to listen to her nonexistent heartbeat. "Okay," she says finally, turning to Vesper. "You can call the morgue. And have the bereavement team notify her parents."

Vesper makes the two calls. In the meantime, Osterman has stepped down into the testing area and is walking around gazing at the subjects. "I know that what you're doing here is very important," he states to Zhu, "but I still don't understand why we had to include minors in this test study." He leans in to get a better look at Beta subject one . . . Catalina.

"Because this test only works on subjects whose brains have not completed myelination," Zhu says, holding BethAnn's limp hand like she never wants to let go. "That's why we only used trial subjects under the age of twenty."

Osterman shakes his head like he doesn't want the words to sink in. "High risk. Bad publicity," he murmurs.

All of a sudden he looks up at me, and stares back and forth at Zhu and Vesper. "What is this . . . person . . . still doing here?"

Zhu looks at me like she has totally forgotten I was here, but Vesper says, "Jaime, premed student at Yale, doing a required internship, was the only witness besides myself to the death of subject three. Jaime is taking detailed notes of everything that happens, which could be quite beneficial if any legal situation were to arise."

Osterman's expression changes from one of scorn to looking like he wants to adopt me. "Jaime . . ." he says, in a buttery tone.

"Salvator," I fill in.

"Jaime Salvator . . . of course. I remember you. You came recommended by one of our most prestigious donors, Ms. Walton-Masters."

I plaster on my smarmiest smile, and that seems to please him. Unsurprisingly, since smarm feeds on smarm.

"If I remember correctly, your mother works for her," Osterman comments, stepping up to the workstation platform.

"Yes, sir," I respond.

"Ms. Walton-Masters told me your story. You won a full-ride scholarship coming from one of Detroit's worst neighborhoods." I can tell from his look that he's wondering if I got it thanks to affirmative action or merit. I feel my smile slipping.

"Jaime is *also* at the top of this year's premed track at Yale," Zhu adds supportively.

"Well, Jaime," Osterman says, standing before me, hands clenched behind his back, "you just let me or my secretary, Jonathan, know if you need any additional information or materials for your research. We have nothing to hide. Everything is open to a promising young rising star like yourself."

"Thank you, sir," I say, giving a weird little seated bow, though I didn't even know my body could do that.

He turns and strides out of the room.

Vesper and Zhu look at each other.

"Who have you talked to?" Vesper asks softly.

"Only three of the parents and legal guardians who had decided to stay . . . the parents of the youngest one, the mother of the narcoleptic, and the aunt of the African boy. We're still trying to contact the others," she says. Hanging her head, she wipes away tears.

"It'll be okay," Vesper reassures her. "This is just a temporary setback." But as his glance sweeps the room and meets my gaze, I see that his eyes are as empty as his words.

CHAPTER 19

CATA

THE SECOND WE HIT THE WALL, I AM BACK INSIDE myself. It's like my spirit fled my body when it was squished up against that dead boy, and though I wanted to get back in . . . needed to get back in . . . I couldn't. My body slammed the door and locked me out. But as soon as I knew I was safely out of there, something cracked open and let me back in.

We've returned to the Void and are heaped in a kind of a pile. Sinclair's lying on the ground on his back, and I'm draped across him, facedown, stomach across stomach, staring at the sole of a brown faux-croc Doc Marten. I crane my neck to see George lying spread-eagle on her back. Fergus has one arm around her leg, and his other hand clenched tightly around my forearm.

"What. The. Hell," George says. It's so quiet here in the Void, compared to the storm we just left outside, that it sounds like she's shouting.

I have two options: roll over Sinclair's head, sticking my boobs in his face, or roll the other way, over his crotch. Both equally compromising. I decide to prop myself up on my hands and knees and crawl off of him, but Fergus has my wrist in an iron grip. "Um, Fergus, if you let go of my hand I might be able to get off Sinclair," I suggest.

"Sorry," he says, and lets go.

"Hey, do you hear me complaining? It isn't every day a cute girl literally throws herself on me," Sinclair says.

I look down from where I'm straddling his chest to see his amusement at my stunned expression. My brain is trying to compute whether or not his remark was flirty, and then I register his cheeky grin. Flirty. Definitely flirty. Which, considering that my crotch is basically in his face, I'm not quite sure how to handle.

George gives a dry laugh. "And he's flirting mere minutes after being dug out from between dead, maggoty bodies and escaping a freaky static monster."

"I don't like to dwell on the past," Sinclair says lightly.

I unstraddle him with as much grace as I can muster. Giving me a teasing wink, he stands and brushes himself off, even though his clothes look as brand-spanking-new as before we got buried alive.

George turns her attention to Fergus. "Getting kind of cozy with my upper thigh, there, are you?"

He turns bright red and untangles himself from her leg. "Only doing what it took to save you from your 'freaky static monster,'" he says, trying hard to sound cool and collected.

"Hey!" comes a voice, and I turn to see Ant scrambling to his feet a little ways away from us, Remi by his side. They make their way over.

"Are you okay?" Remi asks, looking worriedly at me.

"I'm fine now," I reassure him.

Sinclair's brow furrows. "Yeah, what happened to you, anyway? I thought you had died there for a minute. Like, panic-induced heart attack, or . . . I don't know."

I hesitate, and then decide to tell the truth. "I dissociated. It happens."

"What's that mean?" Fergus asks.

"When something horrible happens . . . sometimes . . . my brain just kind of checks out. Leaves."

"She had to roll over a dead guy and got her face stuck up against his," Remi explains to Ant. "There were maggots on her mouth," he whispers.

I shudder violently and Sinclair wraps his arm around me. "We're okay now," he says. His hug feels like an afterthought, like it's something he thinks he should do instead of it coming naturally. But I'll take any kind of comfort right now, so I lean my head on his shoulder. He squeezes once and lets me go.

"That happens to me sometimes," Remi says, breaking the silence. "The disassociation thing. My doctor said it's a symptom of my post-traumatic stress disorder."

He has PTSD too? I think, and then just as quickly remember that he survived a genocide. Of course he does. How could he not?

He had to deal with war . . . with automatic weapons and murder. The source of my PTSD isn't as obvious. It's the outcome of my messed-up childhood. One that no one believed besides a school counselor, a judge, and my dead mom's best friend. It didn't help that my brother and sister told the police I was lying. *He forced them to,* I think. *It's the only way he could keep them.* For the hundredth time I forgive them. *It's not their fault.*

I turn my thoughts back to Remi, and something clicks in my mind. We both have PTSD. Ant is . . . whatever he is. BethAnn was obviously anorexic, besides there being this sadness about her that seemed almost physical. Fergus seems pretty balanced besides his low-blood-sugar fainting thing. But when something stressful happens, he fiddles with his mysterious tattoo, which makes me wonder what the story is behind that. That leaves George and Sinclair, and I'm not totally convinced they're one hundred percent "normal." Most of us here have problems. It feels like a clue.

I tuck it away to think about later, because Fergus is talking. "We got separated. Again. But it wasn't as far away as in the African place."

"So it looks Cata's hand-holding strategy could be right on . . . if everyone can manage to do it." Sinclair raises an eyebrow at Ant.

"I'm not the one who ran away," Ant says, crossing his arms

and tossing his head in a way that makes the dangling strings from his earflaps wave back and forth. "I just let go."

Fergus pats him on the back. "It's okay. That door thing freaks me out too. Not to mention what we might find behind it."

"It's too loud, and I had to cover my ears," Ant says, tapping on his leg four times, and then checking his pulse.

Remi rolls his eyes so violently you can practically hear it.

"Listen, it doesn't matter," George says. "We have less than twenty minutes to figure out what's going on and get ready for the next nightmare."

"How are we supposed to figure out what's going on?" I ask. "Nothing here makes any sense."

George shakes her head. "It's not total anarchy. We already know that there's a fixed-time thing. Ant? You've figured out how long we stay in the Void. What about the nightmares? Has that been the same each time?"

"Around fifty minutes," he says to her and then, gazing around at us, flinches uncomfortably from being the center of attention. "At least it was the first couple of times. This time I wasn't able to keep track."

"That last one seemed a lot longer," I say.

"Probably because we were in a coffin with three rotting corpses," Remi responds. He doesn't look as traumatized as I feel. Maybe because he's used to being around dead bodies.

"So we do have some rules," George says, and holding up a hand, starts counting on her fingers. Thumb: "Twenty minutes in the Void, then fifty minutes in the nightmare." Index finger:

"Our proximity in the Void affects how we land in the nightmare." Middle finger: "However dirty or injured we are in the nightmare, we start from square one again in the Void."

"Unless we're dead," adds Remi.

"And not exactly square one," Sinclair interjects, and, reaching into his back pocket, he holds up the keys that he got off the dead kid in the coffin. "I brought these back from the nightmare. So we don't *literally* start from scratch every time."

Everyone stares at the keys like they're cast in solid gold instead of aluminum or whatever they're made of.

"We can bring things back and forth!" says Ant, awestruck.

"And apparently George here is capable of costume changes," Sinclair says, and then holds his hands up defensively as George directs an evil gaze at him.

"Yeah, you never told us how you did that," I say.

George just shrugs. "I didn't really think about it," she responds. But there's something in her tone that suggests she knows more than she's telling.

"Sinclair brought something back from the nightmare. George can unconsciously change what she wears. That would imply that we have some kind of control," Fergus says, and everyone falls quiet.

"Prom gown," I say, and, holding my arms out from my sides like Cinderella, I look down. I'm still wearing my jeans and tennis shoes. I look up and meet Fergus's gaze. "Just testing."

"Maybe you need a certain level of concentration," Fergus suggests. "Or feel really strongly about it."

"That reminds me of something else," I say. "Remember when we were in the pitch-black Void at the beginning and someone said, 'I wish there were light,' and suddenly the lights went on? Who was that?"

Ant raises his hand tentatively.

"How did you do it?" I ask.

He taps on his leg four times and whispers something under his breath. We all wait, watching his lips move as he stares intently at the ground.

I glance over at Remi. He's closing his eyes, making a visible effort to control his impatience.

Ant clutches his hands together and starts chanting something indecipherable. I go over to him and put my hand on his shoulder. "What are you saying, Ant?" I ask softly.

"Periodic table of elements," George suggests. She's obviously better in chemistry than I am, since I didn't recognize any of it.

"It helps me concentrate," Ant whispers.

Sinclair slips the keys back into his pocket, shaking his head in dismay. "So, *do* you remember how you did the light thing?" he prods Ant.

"I just really wanted it to be light. I hate the dark."

"So maybe you were feeling kind of panicky?" Fergus suggests.

Ant nods his head.

"Maybe it takes a strong emotion . . . or intense concentration. That could be the key," Fergus says, rubbing his tattoo.

Still whispering elements under his breath, Ant stares at Fergus like he's considering what he said and then lowers himself to the floor to sit cross-legged. He closes his eyes and lowers his head like he's praying, his back hunched like it's a shell protecting him from the rest of us. And when he sits back up, he is holding a little leather notebook and a pen in one hand.

"No. Way!" exclaims Sinclair.

Ant releases a huge sigh of relief, like he's been holding his breath this whole time. With his free hand, he taps six times on the ground. "Six," he says. "I needed six things. The hat and gloves and . . . Four isn't enough."

George gives us all this look. "Looks like we can make stuff we need," she says.

I correct her. "Ant can. My prom-dress experiment didn't go so well, remember?"

"Yeah, but did you really mean it?" George asks. "What emotion did you have when you wished?"

"Sarcasm, definitely. Curiosity, maybe," I admit.

She smiles a quirky smile. "That might not be enough."

Silence covers the group like a lead blanket, and I imagine we're all wishing for one thing or another. But nothing else appears like Ant's magic notebook. Meanwhile, he has opened it and is scribbling away, stopping from time to time to click the pen six times before continuing. George herds us away and says, "Let's leave him alone and go talk. We can figure this thing out, I'm sure of it. At least we can figure *more* of it out."

As we walk away from Ant, Sinclair sidles up to me and drapes his arm companionably around my shoulder. He leans in to speak quietly enough that no one else can hear, which in the silence of the Void means he's practically whispering.

"So . . ." he begins, "don't you think George is ordering people around a bit too much?"

I lift my eyebrows in surprise. "Well, she's good at organizing and directing conversation, but I wouldn't say she's ordering anyone around."

Sinclair shrugs. "I mean, you were the one who came up with the holding-hands-as-we-went-through-the-door idea. She hasn't actually come up with anything useful."

"We're all working together on this. It's not like there are teams," I say, nudging him playfully.

"Well, if there were, I'd want to be on yours," he says, squeezing my shoulder. His breath tickles my ear.

"Do you want to know what I think?" I give him an impish smile. "I think you're sore that George gave you the brush-off, and so you're: one, trying to get back at her, and two, giving it a try with me."

Sinclair throws his head back and laughs. "My response to that is: one, you're more perceptive than you look, and two, do you blame me for trying?"

I shake my head in mock dismay. "You are such a player. I don't blame you because I don't take you seriously. But at the very least it's entertaining." *And the hugs and attention aren't bad either,* I think.

He looks pleased with that reply, and, lowering himself to the ground next to where Fergus, George, and Remi have sprawled out, he pats the spot next to him for me to sit.

"So we have twenty minutes in the Void to plan, and fifty minutes in the nightmare to survive," Fergus begins.

"I wish it were the other way around," Remi says.

There is a general murmur of agreement.

"We know we can count on certain things being the same every time," I say. "There are always three knocks before we change worlds. Here in the Void, the blue door appears, and it doesn't matter where we're standing . . . we get swept into it. In the nightmares it's the Wall, but each time, we've had to run to get there."

"It's like the Dreamfall wants to trap us in the nightmares," George says. "We have no choice about going into it, and then have to struggle to get out."

"Maybe it's trying to kill us," Sinclair says darkly.

"Or test us," I suggest.

"The only other thing that's been the same in all of the dreams is that static monster that shows up each time," Remi states.

"Yeah, what's that about?" Sinclair asks. "It shows up right before the Wall appears and tries to keep us from going in."

"Well, if the Dreamfall's trying to trap us inside the nightmares, maybe the monster is part of it . . . like an extension of it . . . It's just another thing making it difficult for us to escape," Fergus says.

"I think I hurt it last time," George says. "Maybe it won't be in the next nightmare. Maybe it will die in between."

"We can only hope," says Sinclair.

"How about the dreams themselves?" asks Remi. He has a

determined gleam in his eye. Like he finally believes some good will come of talking through things. "The last one . . . I mean before the graveyard . . . took place in my town. The Dreamfall must have pulled that from my mind. What about the other dreams?"

There's another contemplative silence.

"Like I said, the cave is mine," Fergus says. "Remember, where we smashed my dad's brains in? And I've been thinking . . . the cave itself could be straight out of a Lovecraft story. I've been reading a lot of them lately."

"Horror lit to go along with your love of horror movies?" George asks.

"I never said I love them," Fergus responds.

"So . . . why?" Sinclair prods.

"Desensitization," Fergus says, rubbing his tattoo. "Don't ask."

Drama queen, Sinclair mouths at me, punctuating it with a wink. Fergus ignores him.

"Whose nightmare is the graveyard?" I ask. "That one's definitely not mine."

Everyone else shakes their head. "Besides the generic horror-movie setting, not mine," Fergus says.

"It seemed different from the others," I continue. "With the genocide and the cave, we were just trying to run away from scary things, human or . . . not. But what was up with the dead kids and all of those weird objects in the coffin?"

"What objects?" Fergus asks. George studies me with that off-putting tilted-head thing she does.

"The corpses were all kids . . . teenagers . . . and they each had something: a knife, a My Little Pony alarm clock, and that set of keys Sinclair was able to bring back. They were holding them in their hands, like they had been buried with them."

"You're talking like they were real people," Sinclair argues. "They're just characters in a nightmare. So what if they were holding weird things? It doesn't have to mean anything."

"Maybe," Fergus says, "but there's also the fact that they were all buried together, and their gravestones all had the same poem. Something about a wolf and honey."

George gets this thoughtful look, directs her gaze toward the sky, and says,

"The traitor spread honey atop pretty lies.
Only the love of his victims he asked.
For deceiving the lamb is the wolf's cherished prize.
And only in death is the true beast unmasked."

"Okaaaaay," says Sinclair, lifting an eyebrow.

"Photographic memory?" I ask.

She nods and shrugs as if it were nothing.

"Wow!" Fergus says, impressed. "So . . . does that remind any-one of anything?"

Another shake of heads.

"Well, I guess we'll have to wait to see if the next nightmare 'belongs' to anybody or if it was just pure chance that one was Remi-specific, and the other belonged to Fergus," George says.

Sinclair lies back on the floor and folds his fingers together across his stomach. "I'm so tired," he moans. "Maybe the best way to get ready for the next nightmare is by taking a nap. If I could just imagine myself up a comfortable bed and a mountain of pillows . . ."

George follows his lead, lying back on the ground, stretching her legs out and crossing her Docs. "I could do with some sleep. Feels like days."

Remi flops back, crossing his hands behind his head. "Sleep? What's that?"

Fergus and I stretch our legs out and lean back on our elbows. I yawn. "You too?" he asks.

"Yeah, I haven't had a good night's sleep in months . . . I mean, I think it's been months."

"It's been years for me," he says.

"Years?" I ask skeptically.

He nods, and this supersad look monopolizes his face. I noticed his eyes before, but in this light their jade hue is striking. They seem to be magnified by his jet-black hair. He has a look on his face like he's trying to decide if he can trust me. He glances at the others, George in particular. Of course, here in the silence of the Void, if he tells me something, everyone will hear it.

"I have narcolepsy," he whispers to me.

"What did you say?" Remi asks.

Fergus glances over at him and sighs.

"Why don't we take a walk?" I suggest.

"Where?" Fergus asks with surprise.

"Um," I say, squinting my eyes, and point to our right. "How about that way?"

He smiles and scrambles to his feet. "Yeah, that way looks good. And it would be nice to walk for once instead of running from something trying to kill us."

"Where are you going?" Sinclair asks. He seems bothered, either that I'm going somewhere with Fergus, or that he's not being included.

"Exercise," I say.

He frowns as we turn and walk away.

George calls, "Don't go too far. If you get lost here, there's no way we'll find each other in the nightmare!"

Fergus sticks his hands in his front pockets and I fold my arms across my chest as we walk, turning every once in a while to make sure the others are still within view.

"I keep hoping that we'll go through a Wall, and instead of the Void, we'll come out in the real world," I say.

"Kind of like in *Time Bandits*," Fergus responds. "When they're in the desert with no end in sight, and they run up against the invisible force field, and one of the little people throws a skull and breaks it, and there's this whole other world just on the other side?" He's looking at me like he expects me to recognize what he's talking about.

"Um . . . maybe?" I say.

"You haven't seen *Time Bandits*?" Fergus asks, gobsmacked.

I shake my head.

"Man, that should be the first thing you do when you get out of here," he says. "Terry Gilliam. Classic."

I glance back and see that the others have become penny-sized shapes floating in the floorless, horizonless white. "We probably shouldn't go much farther," I say. I stretch my hands up above my head and lean far to the left and then to the right, feeling my muscles ache as I do. Fergus rubs his shoulders with his hands and moves his head from side to side.

"Even though we don't bring injuries from the nightmares into the Void," I say, "I still feel like I just ran a marathon and climbed Mt. Everest."

"I know," Fergus says. "And I'm just as tired as I ever was."

"Because of your narcolepsy?"

He nods. "Not everyone with narcolepsy suffers from insomnia, but lucky me—I got the whole package." As he speaks, the circles under his eyes seem to darken.

"I've heard of narcolepsy, but I don't actually know what it means," I admit. "Is it when you fall asleep without warning?"

"That's part of it. I'm always really tired. I nod off during the day, and have a hard time sleeping at night. I have these freaky hallucinations while I'm sinking into sleep and waking back up. And I have cataplexy, not low blood sugar. It's the passing-out thing. Your muscles just give out and you fall over and can be unconscious . . . or not."

"That sounds like it sucks," I say.

"You can't imagine," he responds. "I was able to start college this year, but have to live at home. I can't drive. Can't go out for sports."

"Why?" I ask.

"Because if I have a cataplectic attack I can hurt myself, or worse, other people."

He holds out his arms and inspects them. "Looks like my bruises didn't make it to the Dreamfall. Usually, I'm black and blue from falling into furniture."

I gasp as I see dark shapes form on his skin. "Look!" I say, pointing.

"Wow!" he says, studying a particularly painful-looking bruise on his forearm. "Okay, that was weird. But yeah, this is what I usually look like."

"God. I'm sorry," I say. "Does it happen when you're really sleepy?"

Fergus shakes his head. "It happens when I have a strong emotion. For most people it's fear, surprise, or laughter. I've been trying to take care of it by desensitizing myself."

"That's why you watch horror movies even though you don't like them!"

"Yeah," Fergus admits. "That's worked pretty well. It's not like I can't be scared anymore, but I've learned how to see pretty gruesome things and keep calm. My own personalized behavioral conditioning routine. But my Achilles' heel is laughing. I haven't found anything to work for laughter. Which is why I got this tattoo."

He holds out his left arm, and I finally get a good look at it. The curving, Gothic script spells out three capital letters: *DFF,* the letters Sinclair had teased him about.

"What's it stand for?" I ask.

"'Don't Fucking Feel,'" says Fergus with an amused grin.

I burst out laughing. "You've got to be kidding me!"

Still grinning, he shakes his head. "If I feel a strong emotion coming on, laughter or anything else, I have that reminder right in front of me. It has saved my ass on numerous occasions."

"Whatever works," I say, smiling at him.

Insomnia . . . and not accepting our situation without a fight: that's two things we've got in common. It makes me feel closer to this tall, handsome boy. Like we're connected. I feel like hugging him, but don't want him to take it wrong, so I just squeeze his bicep in a more acceptable you're-okay kind of gesture.

He returns it, brushing my arm with his fingertips before glancing back at the others. "I can't tell time using my pulse, but we should probably start back," he says.

We walk in silence for a moment. "You know what you said about the scary hallucinations you have when you're falling asleep?"

Fergus nods.

"Well, I have night terrors."

"I've heard of that," Fergus says. His dark hair flops down as he walks, hiding his big green eyes. "Do the terrors keep you from sleeping?"

I nod. "They don't help. I don't sleep too well anyway, but when you know you're going to have some skinless, bleeding monster chasing you as soon as you close your eyes, you learn not to close them."

Fergus turns toward me. "I saw that!" he says excitedly. "The first time I saw you. You were being chased by this zombie kind of thing. But much faster than the regular Hollywood zombies."

"I call him the Flayed Man," I say, trying not to let the image take form in my mind. "It's one of the more frequent recurring dreams I've had for the last few years."

"Lucky you," Fergus says sardonically, dipping his head and looking at me sideways. I must look pretty traumatized, because he throws an arm around my shoulders and pulls me in toward him, giving me a side-hug before releasing me. "I guess that coffin dream probably didn't help things, with the dead kids and the maggots."

I shake my head. "I've had worse."

"Worse?" Fergus exclaims. "That's already pretty bad."

Not worse than real life, I think, but of course I'm not going to say that to him. He seems like the kind of guy who's a good listener. And I haven't talked about those things to anyone except Barbara and my shrink. And the school counselor, of course. But she's the reason I am where I am. She told someone else. And that set the wheels in motion.

We're almost back to the others when Fergus says, "Wait. You have night terrors. I have narcolepsy. George and Sinclair and Remi all said something about not sleeping. What if this is the thing?"

"What thing?"

Fergus muses. "What if this has something to do with why we're all here. It's the only thing we seem to have in common so far." He picks up his pace, and we're practically jogging by the time we get back to the others. They're all still lying in a semi-circle, not talking. They'd be staring at the ceiling if the Void had one. As we approach, they turn to look at us.

"Do all of you have problems sleeping?" Fergus asks excitedly.

After a beat of silence, George says, "What?"

"Sleeping! Do you have sleep disorders? I have narcolepsy. Cata has night terrors. Do you guys have anything like that?"

George admits, "I have insomnia."

"Night terrors and insomnia," Remi replies, like they're items on a shopping list and not tools of torture.

Sinclair looks worried. "Insomnia."

Fergus turns to look over to where Ant was sitting, but the boy is standing right behind us. "Do you have insomnia, Ant?" Fergus asks him. Ant looks thoughtful and nods. "I don't sleep much," he admits.

"We all have insomnia," Fergus says, holding out his hands as if offering a gift. "That's got to mean something. It's got to be a key."

"Or else the Dreamfall has a sense of humor," Sinclair says. "None of us can sleep in the real world, but here we're trapped in a nonstop series of nightmares?"

"Maybe your fictional game players get their thrills from torturing groups of insomniac teenagers," George says to Sinclair.

Something blooms on the edge of my consciousness. Something about game players and a group of teenagers. It lingers for a second and then, as quickly as it came, disappears.

"Well, we'll have to figure it out later," says George. "Because we only have a few minutes until the next night—"

Before she can even finish, the first knock comes. Everyone scrambles to their feet. The air around us seems to dim a little as the blue lines begin glowing off to my right.

We all look at each other, and Ant holds out his hands with an expression of distaste, like it's offensive to touch another human being. *Except for George,* I think. *And they're practically joined at the hip.*

"Let's lock arms this time," George suggests. "It will be harder for the wind to rip us apart."

Everyone steps in a bit, and one by one we link arms until we're standing side by side, pressed tightly against one another. The second knock splits the air around us, and the wind picks up, levitating my hair and blowing it into my eyes. I shake my head without letting go of Fergus and Sinclair, and see the door creaking slowly open.

"Hold on tight!" I yell. "We have to stay together this time!"

The wind is blowing so hard it's hard to stand, and our circle leans and stumbles to one side. And then we tilt so far over that it seems like we're falling. The wind scoops us up and we are gone.

CHAPTER 20

JAIME

TRIAL SUBJECT FIVE'S NAME IS REMI AMADI. HE'S
fifteen years old, and is a political refugee from Matangwe, a for-
mer French colony in Africa.

There are photocopies of US government documents showing a passport photo of a scared-looking boy with short-cropped
hair. The forms say he entered the US on February 5 and list his
sponsor as an aunt who lives in Minnesota and works as a nurse.

There is a case summary from a Minneapolis social worker:
"Remi's village was destroyed last year on Christmas Day by anti-
government rebel forces. His entire family was gunned down in
front of him in his house. Remi survived by playing dead, and was
found pinned under the body of his older brother by an international rescue organization that swept the village the next day. He
was relocated to a refugee camp until his aunt came to retrieve him.

"Remi suffers from post-traumatic stress disorder, which manifests in night terrors, insomnia, and hyperrealistic flashbacks. He deals with survivor's syndrome and has expressed crippling guilt for not being able to save his family."

This is followed by a few pages of notes by the psychiatrist who recommended Remi for Zhu and Vesper's trial.

I set the file down, thoughts roiling, something nagging at the edge of my consciousness. The lab door swings open and two white-coated nursing assistants enter, rolling a gurney between them. They pause, looking to the doctors for instruction. "She's over here," Vesper says, and steps down from the monitoring station to walk over to BethAnn.

Working carefully, the men unzip a body bag laid out on the gurney and transfer her limp body from the bed into the bag, zipping it up around her. They take the copy of the death certificate from Vesper, place it in a clear pouch on the top of the body bag, and give him another document in return, which all three men sign. This little ceremony seems to seal the deal. The nursing assistants are basically giving the doctors a receipt for a corpse.

I glance back at the open file in front of me, and something catches my eye that I hadn't noticed before. A red stamp at the top of the photocopied government political refugee document spells out in capital letters "GENOCIDE."

An ice-cold finger runs its way down my spine. That's what BethAnn was talking about before she died. She said something about Africa, being shot by soldiers, and then she actually used the word *genocide*. Could that be a coincidence? This boy's dreams must be replete with men with guns. With genocide.

My thoughts are racing. There is something going on here that is way beyond what Zhu and Vesper assume. I'm sure of it. The secondary symptoms of REM sleep showing up during the fifty-minute cycles. The complete lack of them during the twenty-minute cycles. Are the subjects dreaming?

If so, things are backward: the test was supposed to be twenty minutes REM and fifty NREM. I wonder if the system crash scrambled things somehow. And based on what BethAnn said, I wonder if this glitch could have also created some sort of link between their minds. That sounds way too crazy to be possible. But what *hasn't* been crazy about this test so far?

I have to know more, but don't even know where to start. Vesper definitely isn't going to listen to me. But maybe if I dig up something else. Maybe if there is another event that makes them doubt their everyone's-in-a-coma theory. Maybe I can actually do something that could help.

Glancing over at the researchers to make sure they're not watching, I log into my Gmail and send a message to a friend who's studying IT at Yale. He's practically a celebrity in the hacker world. He's even done stuff for Anonymous. *Hal, I need something urgently. Will pay you in game tickets, whiskey . . . whatever I can snag from friends. Could you give me anything you can on these names . . . especially this one with a locked police file?*

CHAPTER 21

FERGUS

SOMETHING IS TUGGING ON MY ARM. AS MY vision focuses, my eyes adapt to the dim light of what looks like an empty cathedral. The place is huge. Like Notre Dame huge. Not that I've ever been to France, but when you see pictures of people standing in it, they look like ants inside a giant's house.

Cata has my right arm linked through hers. Ant has clamped on to my left, determined not to make the same mistake he did last time. Remi is on his other side, eyes screwed tightly shut. George is distractedly trying to extricate herself from Remi and Sinclair as she gawks upward at the domed ceiling. Sinclair peers around, squinting to see in the dark space. But Cata's expression is different from the others. Eyes wide, she focuses on the far end of the church. There, an altar is lit by an aura of light that seems to radiate from behind it, backlighting two enormous bouquets of dark flowers, one on either side.

"What's wrong, Cata?" My voice comes out in a whisper.

"Mine," she says in a soft voice. "This dream's mine."

"Is it bad?" George asks.

"The worst."

For the first time, George looks worried. This place is pretty spooky. She sees me watching her. "I don't like churches," she says.

"I don't like *this* church," Remi says. Now that he's opened his eyes, they're traveling over every inch of the space, mapping out our new prison, probably strategizing for our survival.

"What's under the purple sheets?" Ant asks in a hushed tone.

Carved into the walls are alcoves furnished with what must be statues hidden under purple satin veils. Opening off of the enormous room we're standing in are smaller side chapels, each with its own altar and statues posed around it, all hung in shiny purple.

"My family's church did that during Lent," Cata explains. "They veil all of the religious objects three weeks before Easter, then on Easter Sunday the coverings are pulled off."

"Like symbolizing they were dead and then come back to life again?" George asks.

"Happy Zombie Jesus Day," mumbles Sinclair, and I flinch.

I guess I'm extrasensitive about mocking other people's religions. It hasn't been easy growing up in a wealthy all-white East Coast town with a Hindu mom from Delhi. Dad's pasty-white-bad-caricature-of-a-Scotsman appearance blended with my mom's striking looks to make me kind of a boring blend of the two. Which means I was never picked on until my narcolepsy got severe. But whenever Mom came to a school activity, I heard people whisper *dot-head* and a few even asked me if she worshipped Buddha. Idiots.

Sinclair notices my reaction. "What? Some ancient guy is dead for three days before busting out of his tomb and scaring the shit out of the soldiers guarding him? Bet he ate their brains, and the Bible just skipped that part."

A jovial smile spreads across his face, but seeing the lack of reaction from Cata, he nears her and puts an arm around her shoulders. "What did I say?" he asks, flashing this totally fake look of sincerity. How can he even think she would fall for that?

"You are such a numskull," George says, glaring at him. "Can't you see this is important to Cata?"

Cata shakes her head. "It *was* important to me. It isn't anymore. Although it's hard to completely forget about it when you've had it shoved down your throat since the day you were born."

"Why are we here?" Remi asks. "What's going to happen?"

"It always starts quiet like this," Cata responds. Her eyes flit from the eerily lit altar at the front to one of the darkened chapels to our right. She shudders. "But the statues will eventually come alive. And then there are the monks with the glowing red eyes."

Sinclair lets out a muffled laugh. "Now, that's original." He shakes his head. "Hey, Fergus. How many of those horror films you've watched had monks with glowing red eyes?"

"None," I say slowly, and raise a quivering finger to point past his left shoulder. "At least nothing like the one standing behind you."

"What the . . ." Sinclair yells as he spins.

George giggles as Sinclair turns back toward me with a sour look. "Ha-ha."

Sinclair is like one of those kids who tries to be jokey with everyone—wants everyone to like them—but never quite gets it right because you can tell it's not sincere. I can't stand that kind of thing. And I can't help showing it.

"The monks are downstairs in the crypt," Cata says, bringing us back to the point.

"Then we'll just be sure to stay out of the crypt." I try my best to sound unruffled by the idea of evil monks in a place of the dead.

Cata shakes her head. "The crypt is the only way to get away from the statues. The cathedral doors are always sealed tight. And I've never found another way out."

"Have you ever actually escaped?" I ask.

She shakes her head. "I'm always running or hiding in this dream. First from the statues and then from the monks. But I always wake up before they get me."

"I doubt we'll have that option this time," George says. "We have to survive for fifty minutes to get back into the Void."

"Forty-nine now," Ant says.

"Okay, this is the first time in the nightmares where we've known what's coming," I say. "Maybe we can actually prepare."

"How?" asks Cata.

"I don't know," I say, looking around. "We could try to find some weapons."

Everyone begins to explore. Unlike in the cave, the place is crowded with objects of all sorts. Heavy candlesticks, large metal crosses, and vases of flowers cover every possible surface, but of course there are no actual weapons. "Just grab anything heavy," I suggest.

"I never tried to fight them off before," Cata says.

"Yeah, but you've always been by yourself, right?" I ask. "This time there are six of us."

She looks uncertain.

I walk three steps away, pick up a skinny brass candlestick that's as tall as my waist, and pry off the fat white candle impaled on a mean-looking metal spike. I hand it to Cata and choose a matching one for myself. They're heavy, but not much more than one of my dad's golf clubs.

Remi is struggling with a larger candlestick, so I trade him. This one is almost taller than I am and feels solid in my hands. If I have to fight moving statues or red-eyed monks, this weapon is about the best I'm going to find.

I turn to see Sinclair empty a bouquet of dead flowers and some putrid green water on the floor out of a three-foot-high copper vase. Holding it by its narrow base in both hands, he swings it like a baseball bat. George walks up with a six-foot pole with a big gold cross stuck on top, and Ant is by her side, holding what looks like a shiny gold dinner plate.

"What are you going to do with that?" Sinclair says, cracking up. "Serve them appetizers?"

Now that he's no longer trying to win over George, Sinclair's obviously not worried about being careful with Ant.

"It's the heaviest thing I can manage," says Ant matter-of-factly.

Sinclair presses his lips together, trying to suppress a laugh.

"Want a cross up the nose, asswipe?" George brandishes her weapon in his direction.

Grasping his vase in one hand, Sinclair holds his arms up in defeat, and, taking a few steps back from her, leans against a marble column as big around as a sequoia. "My motto's always been *don't anger the band chick holding a cross on a stick.*"

"That's funny," George replies, looking up at him, since he's a good five inches taller than her. "My motto is *don't hurt people who are smaller than me.* Lucky for me, you don't qualify."

"Forty-four minutes," Ant whispers.

"Where do we go, Cata?" I ask.

"Um, I think they're coming to us," she says, her face as white as chalk. She nods her head toward Sinclair, focusing on the shadows behind him.

"Yeah, right. I'm not falling for that again." He turns back to George and says, "Listen, sorry for laughing at your protégé. Truce?"

George responds by swinging her cross high into the air and, with a scream that freezes the blood in my veins, brings it down in a powerful arc toward Sinclair's head.

"Holy shit!" he yells, and ducks. George's huge gold cross

connects with a stone figure that has lurched out from behind the column. Long gray fingers tipped with razor-sharp finger-nails slash at Sinclair before George's staff smashes the stone arm to the floor.

Sinclair stares down at his torn shirt. Blood blooms crimson across the sleeve of the yellow button-down at the level of his bicep. He looks back up at his attacker—a stone statue of what looks like a homeless guy with a long beard dressed in Bible-era rags—and lifts his vase to attack it, but it sweeps out with its remaining hand to slice the underside of his lifted arm. Sinclair screams and falls back.

"Knock it over!" I yell and, dashing forward, swing my candle-stick back and aim low behind its legs. Seeing what I'm trying for, George lunges forward with the cross and shoves the statue hard in the chest. The thing stumbles, my stick smashes against its calves, and it reels for a second before toppling over backward. The statue shatters into a hundred chunks of jagged stone against the hard marble floor of the cathedral.

Cata, Remi, and Ant watch, petrified. "Are they all like this?" I call to Cata.

"Pretty much," she says, her voice shrill with panic as she low-ers into a defensive posture, holding her candlestick aloft. From all of the niches in the walls and the side chapels, figures draped in purple cloths begin moving forward into the nave. Cata points a finger at a life-sized figure inching toward us from across the space. Its giant wings are spread wide, a sword held upright with both hands, and a purple cloth draped over its head past its shoulders, hiding the face. "The angels are the worst," she gasps.

"What do we do?" asks Remi, his voice quaking with fear.

George has taken a defensive stance next to Sinclair, who is holding his wounded arm and cursing.

"Well, five and a half of us aren't going to be able to take on"—I glance around and venture a guess—"fifty animated statues with claws like bowie knives."

Ant stands there wide-eyed, holding his plate like a Frisbee. "Where's the crypt?" he asks Cata.

"This way!" she says, and, scooping up her candlestick, sprints toward the front of the church.

The angel is halfway across the nave and is waving its sword in jerky movements like a stop-motion character. "Go!" I yell, and the rest of us run full tilt behind her.

Halfway there, Remi has to use his candlestick to beat back what looks like a rabid stone wolf that has been stealthily circling the periphery of our group. Statues are closing in on both sides, and the angel is bringing up the rear. The purple cloth has finally fallen off his head, showing curly Michelangelo's *David* hair paired with evil-looking eyes and bared, pointed teeth.

Something lunges from our right, cutting Sinclair and me off from the rest of the group: a saint whose mournful eyes are directed toward the ceiling as he nears. What looks like real blood drips from perfectly round stone holes in the centers of his palms and feet, pooling on the marble floor as he moves silently toward us. Slowly, his eyes lower and focus on me, and his hands reach forward, clawing the air.

"Trip him!" I yell to Sinclair as I raise my candlestick.

Sinclair scrambles behind him and braces his leg behind the hem of the long robe while I rear back and ram the pointed end of the candlestick into the saint's chest. The statue topples and falls, but hits the ground in one piece and slowly begins to levitate upward, rising back into a standing position.

Sinclair takes his vase in both hands and starts bashing the thing in the head over and over again, so quickly and with so much force that I am stunned by his transformation from slacker joker to gladiator wannabe. "You got it!" I yell as the thing's head smashes into fragments and the body collapses to the ground. "Let's go!"

We run, dodging statues, to catch up to the others.

"Hurry!" yells Cata. She has pried a large brass grate up from the floor in front of the altar, revealing a stone stairway descending belowground. "Don't wait for us, just go!" I yell, and she disappears into the darkness of the crypt, followed by Remi and Ant.

George waits for us, hunkering in the stairway until Sinclair scrambles down past her. "We have to pull the grate closed," she says. I look back to see that the angel is just a few paces away, and the rest of the zombielike statues have grouped around and are slowly crouching, arms outstretched toward the entrance of the crypt. The two of us grab the heavy metal grill and strain to pull it back into place above our heads. Almost immediately, stone fingers are sticking through the holes in the grate, clawing and scrabbling at the metal.

"Duck," George says. I crouch down as she sweeps the metal icon across the bottom of the grate, chopping off marble fingers and hands, which fall to the stairs and bounce their way to the bottom. George flips the staff around backward and forces the pointed end of it through a gold ring in one end of the grill, all the way across, wedging it into a hole drilled into the stone on the other side.

She looks at me, panting from exertion. "That should do for now."

"You are so incredibly kick-ass," I say, and then immediately regret it. But George gives me an amused smile instead of the scowl I was expecting, and punches me lightly on the arm. "You're not too bad yourself."

Our warm, fuzzy moment doesn't last long. From the darkness below, a scream pierces the air.

CHAPTER 22

CATA

I HAVE HAD THIS DREAM BEFORE. I RECOGNIZE the cathedral, and the freaky angel statue. I remember once running to the massive front doors and finding them bolted closed and the angel baring his fangs and swiping at me with his stone sword, ready to cleave me in two. I was saved that time by my alarm clock going off for school, waking me at the very moment I knew I was a goner.

And another time, I started closer to the front altar, saw the statues coming for me, pushed aside the grate, and flung myself down the stairs into the crypt. Zombielike monks were waiting for me, and I had to run through endless tunnels and hide behind rotting wooden doors to escape them.

But, although I recall certain details with clarity, the rest is foggy. I don't know which way to lead the group. I'm not sure what happens next. And there Remi and Ant are, watching me like I'm going to protect them. Sinclair comes barreling down the stairs while George waits for Fergus, and the two of them work together to secure the grate so the statues can't come down.

"Which way?" Sinclair asks, breathing hard. His arm is hurt, blood soaking his shirtsleeve, but he doesn't seem to notice.

"Come on." I lead them down a tunnel wide enough to drive a car through. Its curved brick ceiling arches just high enough over our heads that we can walk upright. Small niches in the wall hold earthen pots with candles inside, and as we pass them, our shadows are magnified giant-sized onto the stones.

The tunnel opens into a large, round room with the same vaulted brick ceiling. It's supported in the center by a pillar that branches out at the top like a tree and is set with burning torches, their flames flickering in spectral shadows across the walls. All around the room are large niches cut in the wall, stacked in columns of four, the lowest raised just above ground level, and the highest touching the ceiling. Each compartment is about seven feet long and three feet high and just wide enough for the bodies that lay stretched out in them, heads to the right, feet to the left. They wear the white robes I've seen before, tied at the waist with a rope. Their hands are folded over their chests, one placed on top of the other, with rosaries dangling down from their gnarly fingers. Spiderwebs laced with dust drape their resting places like curtains.

"Have you seen this before?" Remi asks.

"Pretty much," I say.

"Who are they?" Ant asks.

"I don't know," I respond. "I've never seen the faces. The hoods are pulled over their heads."

"And they're going to get up pretty soon?"

I turn to the three boys. "Honestly," I admit, "I don't remember how this works. I remember running from these hooded guys. But I don't know if it's these dead monks, or if there are others that come in. It's all really fuzzy."

"Is there any other way out of here besides the way we came?" Sinclair asks.

"A door," I say. "There's always a door. But I don't see it now." My voice is quivering. I know what's coming.

Sinclair takes my hand and squeezes it supportively. "I'm here for you," he says.

His reassurance, not to mention the comfort of his touch, makes me braver. I squeeze back gratefully and walk past him to the far end of the round room, where there is a space between the niches in the wall that could be large enough for a door. Sinclair joins me, and, setting our improvised weapons down on the floor, we begin running our fingers over the dusty white rock. It flakes like chalk under our touch. It seems to have been plastered over, and the plaster is so old that it crumbles away. The outline of a door begins to appear, low enough that we would need to duck to get through it.

"Hey, Cata," Remi says. "This one looks new."

I turn to see the boy crouching near one of the corpses, but far enough away that if the thing woke up it couldn't reach him.

He's right—a few niches in the area are missing the dust and spi-derwebs that make the others appear to have been untouched for centuries.

I lean down to look at the face half-hidden under the lowered cowl. And there, lying in the crypt of the cathedral, dressed in monk's robes, is my father.

I scream.

Pressing my shaking hands to my mouth, I stumble back until I feel a strong arm encircling my shoulder, and I bury my head in Sinclair's chest. "Who is it?" he asks, pulling me close to him.

"My dad," I say, and turn to get a second glance. The thing has my father's white goatee and eyebrows. It has his potato-shaped nose. And the eyes, which are open and staring at the top of his niche, are the same icicle blue. But instead of the rope that the other corpses wear, my father's waist is encircled by a wide leather belt that I recognize all too well. It is the razor strap he used on me almost every day since I was ten. Its brass ring that he used to hang it on the wall by the kitchen table shines in the light of the torches. That small, perfectly round circle had been imprinted in red welts on my skin so many times, it felt like a part of me.

And then my gaze falls to the compartment below him and I double over in Sinclair's arms. "Mom," I gasp.

Fergus and George charge into the crypt, with Fergus bran-dishing his candlestick menacingly. "What's wrong?" Fergus asks. "What happened?"

"It's Cata's parents," Sinclair says, letting go of me with one arm so that he can point out their niches.

I look back up and see my brother and sister lying one above the other in the niches to the left of Mom and Dad. "No!" My voice comes out in a sob, but my eyes are dry. I am numb with sorrow. With fear. With *guilt*. And upon that thought, my sister begins to move.

She slowly swings her legs out of her niche, leaning over as she scoots out of the resting place and stands, facing me with eyes that slowly shift from gray blue to red. And then the red begins to pour from her eyes down her cheeks. Tears of blood flow down her face and stain her white robe as she raises a hand to point at me.

"You killed us," she says. Julia is twelve, but the voice coming from her lips is that of a much smaller child. "Catalina. It's your fault. You shouldn't have told."

Sinclair lets go of me and scrambles for the hidden door. "Help me out," he calls to the others. "There's a door behind here. Only way out." Fergus joins him and uses the pointed end of his long candlestick to start hacking away at the plaster. George picks up my candlestick and holds it like a barrier between Julia and me, looking ready to whack my sister if she comes any closer.

"Watch out!" Ant says. He and Remi have backed away and are standing in the middle of the room with their backs to the central column. I glance away from Julia to see what they're looking at. All of the corpses in the room are slowly easing their way out of their niches. The hoods fall so low over their faces that you can't see anything but a red glow coming from beneath the white linen.

"Faster, Fergus!" George yells.

The boys have the plaster off the door and are scraping off an old keyhole. "We need a key," Sinclair yells. "Where's the key?"

"I don't remember needing a key before," I yell. My sister has grabbed George's weapon with both hands and, with a strength that belies her small build, is shoving the bigger girl back toward me. The hooded corpses are now all out of their niches, shuffling toward the middle of the room where Remi and Ant cower. With the exception of Julia, my family stays motionless, dead in their niches.

"The keys from the casket," Ant says.

"That's right!" George says. "Sinclair, try the keys that you took from the corpse in the graveyard. They must have been there for a reason."

Sinclair stares at her for a moment like she's crazy, then fishes the keys out of his pocket and crouches down near the keyhole. "They're too small," he calls. "The keyhole is for one of those big old-fashioned keys."

"Then kick it in!" George yells. Julia gives the candlestick another violent push, and George shoves her backward so hard that my sister falls into a crumpled heap against the side of the crypt. George turns toward me. "Sorry," she says, and then swings at an anonymous corpse that is closing in on the boys.

I grab one of the torches from the central pillar, slide it out of its socket, and sweep it from side to side to fend off the slow-moving figures. They are all headed toward Sinclair and Fergus, who are delivering powerful kicks to the small door. A low hum comes from all around the room, growing louder every second. It isn't until I smash one of the figures in the chest and his robe catches on fire, sending him thrashing backward screaming, that I realize the hum is coming from the monks themselves.

A cry comes from behind me, and I turn to see that one of the creatures has grabbed Remi and is dragging him toward an empty niche. Remi is struggling so hard that he knocks the cowl back off the creature's head, exposing a zombielike head, flesh hanging from the skull, the hollow eye sockets set with glowing red coals. "Let go of me!" Remi screams.

And then something whizzes through the air, flashing gold in the light of the torches. Ant's plate strikes the neck of the corpse holding Remi, and slices through so smoothly that the body stays erect for several seconds while the head rolls cleanly off and topples with a sodden thud to the floor. Remi struggles with the headless corpse until it too falls to the ground.

I gape at Ant, who, seeing me looking, shrugs humbly and hides behind George, who is fighting like a madwoman to keep that side of the room's corpses at bay.

A sound of splintering wood drowns the humming corpses, and with a final powerful kick, Fergus and Sinclair have smashed the door outward. "Come on!" Fergus yells, and, lunging for where Remi stands covered in the headless monk's blood, tugs him to the door and pushes him through. He turns and drags Ant through the door, sending Sinclair after them. "Come on,

George!" he yells, and she retreats, dropping the candlestick, and ducks through.

"Cata!" Fergus says. I realize that I'm standing there paralyzed, torch in hand, staring at my family's bodies as the dead monks regroup and start back toward us. And as I stare, my father blinks, turns his head slowly toward me, and opens his chalk-white lips. "Everything I did was because I loved you," he says. "And you betrayed me."

"No!" I cry, holding the torch in front of me like a shield as he swings his legs over the edge of his niche and begins to stand.

"Come on!" Fergus yells, brandishing his candlestick in one hand, and with the other shoving me through the doorway into the space beyond, where a stone stairway curves upward in what seems like an endless spiral.

I hear him take a whack at my father and yell over my shoulder, "Don't hurt him, Fergus!" *Where did that come from?* I ask myself. I spent years wanting to get back at him. To hurt him as much as he had hurt me. And now I'm trying to protect him?

"Go," Fergus says from right behind me, and we begin dashing upward. I see the others in front of us, taking the stairs two at a time, running as fast as they can.

The humming is coming from beneath us now, rising in pitch, and I glance back to see a white-robed figure step into the stairway, far below us. "Go faster!" Fergus yells to the others. "They're following us."

We run up the spiral stairs for what seems like forever—my

heart is beating out of my chest, and my head is spinning with the sharp curves—until suddenly we are standing on a balcony inside the cathedral, a mind-boggling height above the ground. The only way for us to take is a narrow walkway with a feeble wood railing running around the circumference of the dome's interior. We are so high that the lit central altar looks like a tiny Lego piece far below. In front of the altar, grouped around the entrance to the crypt, are a dozen minuscule white shapes: the statues, waiting motionless for us to come out. I shiver, not knowing which is creepier, the monks or the statues.

The walkway is only wide enough for one person, and Sinclair, Remi, Ant, and George are lined up side by side, backs pressed firmly against the wall. I scoot next to George to leave room for Fergus.

"Whoa," he says, as he emerges from the stairway, wobbling as he comes to a quick stop. He looks slightly sick as he peers over the edge.

The humming noise is getting louder. "Those things are coming up the stairs," Fergus says.

George leans forward, scoping out the walkway. "There's another door on the far side. We'll have to get over to it. It's the only other way out that I can see."

"Then let's go!" Fergus says. Sinclair unglues himself from the wall and begins walking carefully, like he's on a tightrope, one hand on the railing and the other pressed to the side of the dome.

"I'm scared of heights," Remi admits.

"Then don't look down," George instructs.

"Famous last words," Sinclair mutters and continues shuffling forward at a snail's pace.

"You have to go faster," Fergus urges, peering nervously behind us as the humming nears.

Following George's advice, I keep my eyes on the space directly in front of my feet, one hand gripping the wood railing and the other pressing the flaking paint of the dome wall.

From behind me, I hear Fergus say, "They're out."

I turn to see one of the white-robed monks race out of the entrance to the stairway and immediately pitch forward over the railing. The body turns head over feet several times before it hits the ground far below with a distant thud, facedown, arms spread out wide.

Sinclair yells, "Holy shit!" and picks up his pace.

I glance back to see another figure emerge from the stairway. The hood is pulled back, revealing my father's face. Blood runs in rivulets from his eyes down his hollow cheeks. He moves more carefully than the previous monk, turning to follow us onto the walkway.

"Your dad, right?" Fergus asks me.

"Yes." My throat clenches with emotion, but no tears come.

"I can't go much farther," Sinclair calls. "There's stuff blocking our way."

He has stopped in front of a pile of tools and paint cans. A rope ladder hangs past the walkway from where it is suspended high up in the dome. One rung is attached with a hook to the railing next to the paint cans, and the interior of the dome around it is white with fresh paint.

"You'll just have to get around it!" George yells from behind him.

Cursing, Sinclair begins to pick up the paint cans and stack them against the wall, trying to clear enough space to pass. Behind us, my father starts humming.

I turn to see Fergus lift the candelabra like a lance and shove it hard through my father's chest. Dad's feet keep moving as he tries to walk forward against the candlestick, while a chrysanthemum of red blooms on his white robe where the sharp tip is buried.

Dad stops humming and makes clawing motions toward Fergus, even though the metal rod separates them by a good six feet.

"Hurry!" Fergus yells. "I don't know how long I can hold him back."

"It's too late anyway," Ant says, his voice impassive.

A deafening boom rocks the cathedral, rattling the windows and shaking the walkway so violently that a section just a few feet in front of Sinclair breaks off and plummets in what seems like slow motion to the floor far below.

I press myself up against the wall and crouch down, bracing myself. Fergus looks over at me with an agonized look. "I'm sorry, Cata. I have to do this." And, shoving his back against the wall, he pivots the candlestick outward, flinging my father over the side of the railing. A lump forms in my throat as my father falls—hissing as he reaches out toward me—but I steady my back against the wall and force myself to watch. As he hits the ground, the black wall materializes in front of us, bisecting the dome. Behind it, the rest of the cathedral disappears.

If we could run around the walkway, we could go right through the Wall into the Void. But the section of the walkway that caved in—just beyond where Sinclair stands—has left a gaping hole in our path, making it impossible to reach. We look at one another, our expressions ranging from dazed to hopeless.

"Can we jump from where you're standing through the Wall?" Fergus calls to Sinclair.

"It's too far!" Sinclair yells back. "There's got to be a good twenty feet between me and it. There's no way we can make that jump."

We all stare at the Wall, the floor, and back to each other. The silence is broken only by the vibration of the stained glass in the windows, which are still rattling from the shock of the boom.

Then George says, "Sinclair! The rope ladder!"

Sinclair looks at her, confused.

"The rope ladder that the painters left. Unhook it from the railing and use it to swing out toward the Wall."

The ladder stretches up to where it disappears through an open trapdoor high up near the pinnacle of the dome and down past us to where it ends a good five feet below the walkway. If it weren't attached to our railing with the iron hook, it would hang straight down the center of the dome, ending in midair. But obviously the workers had been using the hook, along with a pull cord tied from the rail to the ladder's bottom rung, to move it around to where they were painting.

I can see what George is suggesting: treating the ladder like a rope swing over a lake. Except, instead of being able to get a running start, Sinclair will be using the wide angle of the rope's position, plus gravity, to launch him out into the space and through the Wall.

Sinclair stares at George, then looks back at the Wall, and then at the rest of us. "No fucking way!" he exclaims.

The second boom is more violent than the first. It is immediately followed by the sound of a million panes of glass breaking simultaneously as the two stained-glass windows beneath the dome explode.

"Do it, Sinclair!" I yell. "It's our only hope!"

Sinclair detaches the rope ladder from the hook and yanks on it to test it. It holds. With ashen face, he grips on to one of the rungs above his head with both hands. "This is crazy," he says. For the first time since he ran off in the Void, he looks seriously frightened.

"Do it!" George says. "Climb over the rail and jump."

Sinclair shakes his head but obeys, slinging one leg over the rail and shoving that heel between the bars holding the rail to the walkway. Slowly, he edges the other foot over, and then, with a shriek of terror, he pushes off. For a second he is falling through space.

Then the rope picks up the slack and he is swinging in an arc toward the Wall. He bisects a column of light streaming through the broken window, and it illuminates his body as he explodes through a cloud of dust motes swirling in its glow. When he gets close enough, he curses loudly and lets go. As soon as he touches the Wall, he disappears.

"It worked!" Remi shouts.

"Grab the pull cord and haul the ladder back," George instructs, shepherding Remi and Ant toward the spot where Sinclair had been standing. Remi grabs it and starts pulling, fist over fist, until he's grasping the ladder in his trembling hands.

"Go. Fast!" George says, and holds on to Remi, steadying him as he climbs atop the rail.

"I can't do this!" he says, looking like he's going to faint.

"You don't have to. I'll push you. Hold on tight, and then let go when you get close to the Wall," George says. And before he can argue, she shoves him hard. Remi goes swinging out into the sparkling dust-strewn air, hits the Wall, and disappears.

George pulls the rope back and says, "Ant can go with me." Cocooning Ant with her body, his arms fastened around her neck and legs circling her waist, she swings the two of them out across the Void and into the Wall.

Fergus and I shift down to their spot and hastily pull the cord back until we have the rope ladder in our hands. As the third boom comes, the inevitable wind arises, whipping out around us from inside the Wall. Fergus shouts, "There's no time left! We have to go together!" He grabs one rung, and I grab the one beneath it. He raises his foot up and kicks the rail hard. The wood disintegrates under the impact and is swept around us by the wind like debris in a tornado.

"Now!" Fergus yells, and we swing through the gap in the rail out into the air over the cathedral floor that is so far away it seems to be worlds beneath us. Just as we near the Wall, something comes flying at us—a barely human form, shaking and flailing like it's suffering an epileptic fit. Blinking in and out of view so quickly it is no more than a blur, the static monster flies at us. It stretches out its claws and swipes wildly at Fergus.

Fergus screams, his head tilting backward, loosening his grip on the rope to bat the thing away. The last thing I see before I'm engulfed by the darkness of the Wall is Fergus wrapped in the monster's arms. Falling.

CHAPTER 23

JAIME

I AM ALMOST SURE NOW THAT THE PERIODS OF heightened heart rates and muscle tension are phases of dreaming for the subjects and that the stable periods are NREM. I have kept a list of the phases—they vary slightly in length, but are close enough to be consistent. If I'm right about this, including the normal twenty-minute REM phase before the system crashed, the subjects are coming to the end of the fifth dream cycle.

I watch as the timer I set on my computer hits fifty minutes, and get ready to jot the time in my notebook. But fifty minutes passes with no change. With a feeling of uneasiness, I watch the numbers climb. Fifty-one minutes. Fifty-two. Could I have been wrong?

I prop my forehead on my hand and think about what an

idiot I've been. Who am I to think I would know more than these researchers who have decades of experience? The phases have probably been a fluke, and I've just been grasping at straws because I want to be able to do something. Not just to look good to Zhu and Vesper, but because I actually want to help.

I begin to shut my notebook, and then I hear the beeping of the monitors decelerate. I look up. It's been fifty-three minutes. That's close enough. I pick up my pen to note the time and activity. And then I realize that the beeping hasn't slowed on two of the monitors.

Subject seven's feedback has never stabilized, staying at the heightened rate this whole time, so that's not odd. But it sounds like this time another subject hasn't stabilized either.

This gets the doctors' attention. They hover around Vesper's monitor for a moment, examining the readouts, and then walk down into the test area and head for Subject two: Fergus.

"He's showing eye movement," Vesper says, "and his heart rate is still elevated."

He's still dreaming, I think.

And, as if she read my mind, Zhu turns to Vesper with a curious expression. "Do you think they might actually be dreaming? You mentioned it before, but maybe I shot you down too fast."

My guess was right, I think, feeling vindicated. But Vesper shakes his head.

"No. dreaming would be impossible with the delta brain waves. I agree with you that what we're seeing is the aftereffects of the interrupted electrical current. Their bodies are obviously working through the shock that it induced."

I feel like butting in. Like showing them the chart I made. But, like a coward, I stay silent and listen as they drop the topic and move on.

"Those aftereffects obviously affected subject three in a way her body couldn't manage," Zhu says with a frown. "What if that happens to one of the others?"

"Subject three's heart might have already been weakened by her anorexia," Vesper suggests. "We'll know more after the autopsy."

"Yes, well, subject seven isn't in the best of health either," Zhu says, glancing at the boy.

"His problem is in his brain, not his heart," Vesper replies, joining her to stare at him. "I never thought I would see one of these cases. There are so few. But he got to you so late. Too late, I'm afraid."

My curiosity is piqued. What could they be talking about? I decide to look at subject seven's file next.

"I don't want to take any more chances," Zhu says, glancing back at Fergus, and then walking back to her station. She picks up her phone. "Yes, this is Zhu in Lab One. I would like six life-support systems delivered immediately, including oxygen and defibrillators."

She gets off the phone and sighs. "By the way, Frankel agreed to a Skype session with us in a half hour. Hopefully, he'll have some ideas."

Zhu and Vesper take their seats and begin going over the events, detail by minuscule detail. Seeing that they are immersed in their conversation, I open the folder to subject seven's file, but am distracted by a flashing icon on my computer screen. It's a new message—from Hal.

Nothing really juicy to flag on most of the names you gave me. Only two of them had police files. The Fergus guy was picked up by the cops a few times, but those were incidents where he passed out or something. One minor car wreck, a few wipeouts including pedestrians on bicycles. Sounds like the guy is massively uncoordinated.

However, was able to get into the NYPD file for Sinclair Hartford, and man, someone could write a novel about this guy's past. The stuff on his regular police file all clicks with Manhattan rich-kid stuff. Minor drug possession, breaking and entering, fights . . . Sounds like the type who knows Mommy and Daddy will bail him out. BUT . . . the locked file. That's where things get interesting.

About three years ago, he was questioned about the suicide of one of his schoolmates. He had been the girl's only friend, apparently, and the day after she died he turned in a suicide note she had given him for her parents "in case." He was reprimanded for not bringing it to anyone's attention in time to save her.

The year after that, he was present at a violent mugging, where another kid from his parents' social club was stabbed to death. Sinclair got away with minor injuries.

And just last year, there was an incident where one of the teenage residents of his building got locked into one of the basement storage spaces and died. The dead kids' parents said he had been hanging around with Sinclair recently. But there was no evidence linking him to the accident, and he had an alibi: he and his parents were out of town the weekend the boy got locked in.

Since nothing came of it, his parents raised a stink and had the judge seal the file in case of future prejudice.

I write back, asking for one last favor.

His response is immediate: *Let me get this right. You want me to hack into this kid's shrink's computer?*

I write him back saying I swear I'll return the favor somehow.

His message back: *Are you kidding? I haven't had this much fun since Anonymous had me track Assange. This one's on me!*

CHAPTER 24

CATA

I LAND IN THE VOID, SPRAWLED FACEDOWN ON the ground, the impact knocking the breath out of me. I look up to see the others struggling to get up. George is already on her feet, her arm around Ant, who is shaking. "Where's Fergus?" she asks.

For a second I don't remember, and then, with horror, I see it again in slow motion, replaying in my mind. "He fell," I say, my voice wavering.

"What?" George stares at me incredulously.

I push myself up and look around at the group. All eyes are on me. "He fell!" I say, and my eyes do that stinging thing that would mean tears if I hadn't intentionally dried them up forever.

"What do you mean he fell?" Remi asks, looking like he's about to burst into tears himself.

"We took the rope ladder together, and just as we were swinging out, that static monster from the other dreams showed up out of nowhere and pulled him off the rope."

"Did you see them land?" Sinclair asks.

I shake my head. "The monster kind of wrapped around him, and Fergus couldn't hold on. I saw them falling when I hit the Wall."

"Shit," says Sinclair.

"I wonder what that means," George says. "I mean, he didn't show up here and then disappear like BethAnn did."

"Yeah, but you dragged BethAnn through the Wall," Remi says. "She disappeared once she was in here. Fergus never even got through."

No one wants to say what all of us are thinking. That Fergus, too, could be dead.

Finally, Remi breaks the silence. "I wonder if the nightmares keep going after we leave them, or if they just disappear. I mean, they're obviously created in our minds. Do they continue playing without us, or do they disappear once we leave?"

"I've been thinking of the Dreamfall as just one place," says George, "where all of the nightmares play like films, one starting where the other ends. Although I suppose each nightmare could have its own world."

"In which case he would be stuck in the cathedral one," I say. "But in your self-contained-nightmare-dimension scenario, the cathedral dream ends and another one starts. So maybe he'll make it to the next nightmare?" As I say it, I realize how just how much this almost-stranger means to me. With what we've been through, I feel like Fergus is already a friend. He can't just be . . . gone.

"That is, if he survived the fall, and those creepy living statues and red-eyed monks didn't get him after that," Sinclair says, giving voice to my fears.

Ant has pulled out his notebook and pen and is scribbling furiously, while still standing. "Hey, Ant," Sinclair says. "You think you could do some of your magic again and conjure us some couches? It might be nice to actually relax for a while before we're sucked into another nightmare."

"It's not magic," Ant replies dryly. "It's visualization while in a meditative state." Everyone turns to stare at him.

"Excuse me?" Sinclair asks, raising an eyebrow.

"I learned to meditate," Ant says. "To control my anxiety." He looks worriedly at Sinclair and then taps six times on his leg.

"Looks like that's worked out really well for you," Sinclair jokes, and then, at a sharp look from me, softens his voice and says, "Magic. Meditation. However it works, would you pretty please give it a try?"

Ant looks at him pointedly for a moment, and then, sitting down with his legs crossed, he closes his eyes and places his gloved palms carefully on his kneecaps. A moment later, a circle of six large cream-colored couches appears beside us. Ant opens his eyes and, for the first time, gives a small, pleased smile.

"No way!" Sinclair exclaims and, jumping onto the nearest couch, sprawls out and puts his hands behind his head. "I can't even tell you guys how good this feels," he moans in pleasure.

We take a couch each and spread out on them. I bask in the comfort of having something soft under my aching back, but can't enjoy it for long. I keep thinking about Fergus and where he might be now. Probably dead. But maybe not. "I know everyone wants to relax," I say finally. "But we've lost two people. We really need to figure out what we're doing here," I say finally. Groans come from around the circle.

George props herself up on an elbow and looks around at the rest of us. "What was it that Fergus was saying about sleep just before we got sucked into the last nightmare?"

"He was pointing out that we all seem to have problems with sleep," Remi says. "He thought that was the one thing that joined us."

"Fergus told me he has narcolepsy," I add, shimmying up into a sitting position so I can see the others. "I have night terrors. And everyone else here has some sort of sleeping problem, right?"

Everyone nods.

"Does anyone take meds for it?" I venture.

Remi shakes his head. "I don't like pills," he says.

"Ambien," Sinclair says.

"Meditation and exercise," Ant says, and George says, "Same for me, more or less."

"Zoloft," I offer and shrug.

"What?" Sinclair says. "Were you thinking this might be a drug-induced communal hallucination?"

"Do you have a better idea?" I respond.

"What about my genius we-got-sucked-into-a-video-game hypothesis?" Sinclair says with a twitch of his lips.

"Cata's right. Let's be serious," George urges. "We all have sleep problems. We're all under twenty. What could have brought us all together and stuck us in this place?"

"Treatment," Ant murmurs, and then sits up suddenly. "Treatment!"

"What?" Sinclair and I ask simultaneously.

"Treatment. I remember my doctor talking about a treatment. It was during my February appointment. Hey! I remember February now!"

"Congratulations," Remi says dryly.

"No, when Fergus asked us before, the last thing I remembered was Christmas. I'm getting my memory back."

"Temporary memory loss," George chimes in. "It means we all suffered a traumatic event: blows to the head, seizures . . . What else causes temporary memory loss?"

"Electroconvulsive therapy." As soon as I say it, the memories come flooding back.

"Oh my God," Sinclair says, sitting up. "It's that experimental treatment my doctor was pitching to my parents and me. A treatment for insomnia."

"That's it!" George says. "I remember my doctor telling us about it. I think it was going to happen in March."

"I don't remember having decided one way or the other because the whole thing seemed pretty extreme," Sinclair says. "Although my parents were really pushing for it, so I wouldn't be surprised if I gave in."

George is snapping her fingers, head lowered, as if she's trying to will the memories back. "It was a beta test. One person had done it before and it had worked."

"Wasn't it based on the electroconvulsive therapy they give for mental disorders?" I ask.

"Yes! And that's known to produce temporary memory loss," George says with a finality that means she's convinced.

"We all went through the test," I say.

"Something bad must have happened," Remi adds.

"Unless this was supposed to be the result," Sinclair responds. "Which I seriously doubt, seeing that two of our group have either died or disappeared. But who knows . . . Maybe fright therapy was a part of the plan." He turns to me. "Fright therapy—my parents would have loved that. Always trying to scare the crap out of me with their empty threats."

He follows this with a bitter smile, unlike the friendly ones he's been giving me so far. It's the first time he's mentioned his parents, and I can't help but wonder what could have happened with them to bring such a cold look to his eyes. And then I think of my own past. Enough evil can be packed into a few years of childhood to mess you up for the rest of your life.

"Okay, what do people recall?" George asks. "Does anyone actually remember doing the test?"

Everyone shakes their heads.

"So we're still suffering memory loss from the actual event. Does anyone remember going to the hospital where it was happening?"

"I remember we were scheduled to attend a meeting one week before it happened. My aunt and I were planning on staying with friends of hers in Larkmont between the meeting and the treatment," Remi says.

"I remember that there was supposed to be a meeting too," I say. The others nod, urging me on. "A meeting with the doctors and the parents and the seven test subjects . . ." My voice wanes as something clicks. "Seven! There were supposed to be seven test subjects!"

Sinclair holds a hand up. "Me . . . you," he says, pointing at me, "Ant, Remi, George, Fergus, and BethAnn. That's seven."

"But . . ." Ant begins, and then shuts up.

"But what?" Sinclair asks. "There are seven of us. We were all supposed to go through a scientific study in March to cure our insomnia. That's got to be it!"

"Then what happened? Is this part of the experiment?" Remi asks.

"Can't be," Ant says. "It doesn't make sense."

"Why?" I ask, but he's busy scribbling in his notebook.

"So what's this mean?" Remi asks.

"Something got screwed up," Sinclair responds. "There's no way this was supposed to happen. From what I remember, the therapy was just supposed to last for six hours."

"It was supposed to be five hours and fifty minutes," counters George.

"Whatever," Sinclair says, brushing off her correction with a shrug. "It already seems like we've been in here forever."

"Maybe it's one of those time-warp things, and we've only been here for a few seconds. And when we wake up it will have worked," I venture.

"No, remember? Ant's been counting," George says, and turning to the boy asks, "How long do you think we've been here?"

Ant taps six times with his pen on his notebook, looks up at George, and then speaks in a voice so soft that we all have to lean in to hear him. "Before we all saw each other, we were in our own individual dreams for twenty minutes. Let's count that as nightmare one. Since then there have been four more nightmares, and this is the fifth Void. At the end of this one, we will have been in here for a total of three hundred twenty minutes."

"Okay, unless the whole thing is time-warped, or Ant's pulse doesn't count for shit," Sinclair says, "we've been here for more than five hours. Which means if we make it through another nightmare and don't wake up after that, we can be sure that the experiment has gone wrong."

"Someone's died. I assume that means it's definitely gone wrong," I say.

"We don't know she died," insists Remi. "She could have woken up on the other side."

"Okay . . . how creepy is this?" I say. "Somewhere all of our bodies are lying in some lab, hooked up to who knows what kind of machines. That includes BethAnn and Fergus, who could be awake or . . ."

"Dead," fills in Sinclair.

"One more nightmare," says George. "If we can make it through just one more, then it is possible that the test will be over and we'll wake up."

"I hope that happens," Sinclair says, "because I want to tell those researchers how messed up their little experiment is. I'd rather never sleep again than have to go through just one of those fucked-up nightmares."

"About the nightmares," says George, "it's pretty clear that each one comes from one of us, and they seem to be alternating. Although we still don't know who the graveyard belonged to." She looks inquisitively at Sinclair, but he shakes his head.

Ant says, "If I've had that dream before, I definitely don't remember it."

"Me neither," George says automatically.

"Could the graveyard have been BethAnn's?" Remi asks.

"Possibly," George says, "if she was still somehow linked to us. She didn't show up in it, though. I guess we can't really know."

"So if the nightmares are rotating through each of our subconscious, one by one, that means the next dream will be either Ant's, George's, or Sinclair's," I say.

"It did help us prepare in the cathedral when you recognized where we were," George says to me. "So, Sinclair . . . what are your worst nightmares?"

Sinclair scratches his chin as if thinking, and then looks George in the eye. "I don't remember my dreams."

"None at all?"

"None."

"Well, that's . . . helpful," she says, frowning. "Ant?"

"The dream I had before the first Void was the one where these invisible people take me to a cabin, tie me to a chair, blindfold me, and start pulling out all of my teeth one by one because I won't tell them the answer."

"I saw you there," Sinclair said.

I nodded. That must have been Ant blindfolded in the creepy room I saw after my Flayed Man dream. "The answer to what?" I ask.

"That's the thing," Ant says. "I don't know the question."

"Do you have any other recurring nightmares?" I ask. "Because my first one, when I was alone, and the cathedral one are dreams I have all the time."

Ant adjusts his gloves and stares at the nonexistent ceiling. "There's one where my bed is in a forest and there's a robber sneaking up on tiptoes to give me a shot in the nose that will make me die. There's one where ghosts with axes are chasing me through a scary house. There's one where poisonous snakes are under my bed, so I can't get out without dying." He counts the dreams off on his fingers. One. Two. Three. I'm surprised he doesn't try to find three more so he can have six, but he only looks at us and shrugs. "I never have good dreams. Except when Dog sleeps in bed with me."

"Dog?" Sinclair asks.

Ant hesitates, looking like he's afraid he's said too much. In a timid voice, he says, "Dog. He's my dog. A rescued pit bull mix."

"And his name is Dog?"

"That's what he is. A dog," Ant says with a tone of defensiveness.

"Your parents didn't name you Child," Sinclair says.

"They let me name the puppy, so I named him Dog," Ant says, looking like he's about to lose his cool. He wraps his arms around himself, and it's clear that that's all he's going to say.

"My dreams are all pretty vague," George interjects. "It would be hard to prepare for any of them."

"So all we've got to do is tackle a robber before he gives Ant a shot in the nose, rescue Ant from the snakes under his bed, or escape from the haunted house without being hacked to pieces by ax-wielding ghosts," Sinclair says. "No problem."

George rolls her eyes. "I think that what we did last time worked pretty well—finding objects we could use as weapons and knowing what we were up against. If we hadn't done that, I'm pretty sure we would have lost more than Fergus in the cathedral."

"We're not sure Fergus is dead," I insist.

"Well, he's as good as," says Sinclair. "He'll be trapped in that creepy cathedral forever."

"No. We talked about this. He could be in the next dream. He could have gotten out of the Dreamfall. Why are you being so negative?" I ask.

"I'm not being negative. I'm being realistic," says Sinclair, shrugging.

Even though I realize he might be right, I don't want to accept it. I give him a frown, and he says, "What?" and reaches out to touch my arm.

George interrupts. "Just . . . stop, you two. Let's think about this. What if we end up somewhere where there aren't weapons conveniently lying around all over the place?"

Everyone is silent for a moment.

"Sinclair, do you still have those keys?" I ask.

He fishes in his back pocket and pulls them out.

"Sinclair brought something from a nightmare into the Void. So maybe we can bring something from the Void into the nightmares!"

"I had my notebook and pen with me in the cathedral," Ant confesses. "They were in my back pocket."

"Oh my God," I say. "Do you know what this means? We could make weapons here and take them with us." This idea seems to energize everyone. "Ant, how did you say you make things appear?" I ask.

"I put myself into a meditative state," he says, "switch my brain off, and then focus on the one thing I want."

"I tried to meditate," Sinclair says. "Couldn't ever do it."

"Ant, could you try to make a sword?" George asks.

"I'd rather have a gun," Remi says.

"Now we're talking!" crows Sinclair.

"Does it have to be a weapon?" Ant asks. "Weapons wouldn't have helped in the cemetery dream. Maybe shovels and a crowbar."

"Ant's right," George says. "Maybe we should think about more useful items. Like rope. A flashlight . . ."

"How about knives? Those can serve all sorts of purposes," says Remi.

"Not quite as much as a semiautomatic," murmurs Sinclair, then he grins when I give him a look.

"Remi is right," George says. "Start small."

Ant shuffles down to the floor, resting his back against his couch. He crosses his legs and places his hands lightly on his kneecaps. A minute passes. Remi looks like he's getting impatient, but George holds a finger to her lips to silence him.

Ant raises his head and opens his eyes, and there on the floor in front of him is a dagger. And not just any dagger. This looks straight out of a museum: a blue-and-gold handle with a fancy leather sheath.

"Holy crap!" Sinclair yells, and scrambles over. Ant holds the weapon out to him, and Sinclair inspects it carefully, his eyebrows raised so high they're practically touching his hairline.

"Not to ask too much," George says, "but can you get one for each of us? If this is the last nightmare, maybe it's all we'll need to survive before we can get out of here."

Within minutes, we are each holding our own dagger, as well as a belt with a sheath so that we can link arms without having to hold our weapons in our hands.

"How much more time do we have?" Sinclair asks Ant.

"Five minutes. No, wait . . . I mean three," Ant says with a look like he's hiding something.

"What's wrong, Ant?" I ask.

Ant looks at George, and they seem to come to a silent agreement. "Ant told me during the last Void that the timing actually isn't completely consistent," George says.

"What does that mean?" I ask.

"I'm not sure yet," Ant responds. "We haven't been here long enough for me to confirm a pattern." Why does he look like he's holding something back? Why would the timing be that important?

"It doesn't matter," George reassures us. "Like Sinclair said, if we're only in here for less than six hours, it might be the last time anyway."

"Okay, then let's plan," Sinclair says. "There are just five of us now. We need to stay together, whatever dream is coming: Ant's or George's."

"Or yours," Remi adds.

Sinclair nods his head, as if that went for granted. "Once in the nightmare, Ant will keep us up-to-date on time we have left, and near the end we'll be ready to make a run for the Wall. Like Cata said, this could be the last time."

Or we could be stuck in here forever. Nobody says it, but we're all thinking it. How long would we survive if we have to continue going up against the freakish creatures populating one another's subconscious?

I wonder if, after a while, I would just give up. If I would choose death over a never-ending wheel of fear and pain. In real life I was able to escape my monsters. *Monster.* But what if I had been trapped there like I am here, knowing I would suffer an endless cycle of torture? What if I had been told I could never leave my home . . . my father? Would I have chosen to die?

In that situation, I was able to escape, but it meant abandoning my brother and sister. Could this time be different? Could I save everyone else along with myself?

This time I'm facing possible death. But what is my life worth if I have to face the world alone?

My thoughts are interrupted by the noise we'd all been waiting for. From around us comes the first knock.

"Come on," George urges, shaking us into action. We group together in our increasingly smaller circle and join arms. Ant pats the dagger at his waist to reassure himself it's still there. Sweat beads on Remi's forehead, and Sinclair licks his lips nervously.

The blue lights appear just as the second knock deafens us. And as the door creaks slowly open, the wind begins to tear at our clothes and hair. "Lock your arms!" George cries over the howling wind, and everyone tightens their hands around the arms they're gripping.

"I forgot one of my dreams," Ant yells. "The worst one!"

"What is it?" I yell back as our group begins to sway and stagger against the gale-force wind.

As we are picked up off our feet and flung toward the door, Ant's words are barely audible. But a chill goes through me when I understand what he said.

The clowns.

CHAPTER 25

JAIME

THE NURSES ARRIVE WITHIN FIFTEEN MINUTES and start setting up a table next to each bed. The subjects already have IVs supplying hydration, but nutrition bags are added. I try not to think about what this means: long-term care. But I can't help wondering if the kids' parents aren't going out of their minds with anxiety.

I know Zhu and Vesper are working on a solution: some way of shocking the kids back into consciousness. What if it doesn't work? What if it kills them? What if it causes permanent brain damage?

I look around at the six subjects lying on the beds and feel a mix of hopelessness and determination. I have this completely irrational delusion that I can do something. That it's up to me to figure out what is going on and find a solution.

A ventilator is also set up next to each subject. Zhu tells the nurses that they don't need to attach them just yet, but she wants them on hand in case "care becomes extended." I notice she doesn't look them in the eyes when she says that. Although she wants to be prepared, she doesn't want to think in that direction.

Finally, a manual external defibrillator is placed on each table, paddles at the ready.

By the time all six life support tables are set up, I hear the beeping of the monitors accelerate and check my clock. Only fifteen minutes this cycle. Something's off. I need to recheck my notes.

Zhu and Vesper take another sweep around the beds to check all vital signs, and then come up to me. "Jaime, Dr. Vesper and I are going to have an emergency video conference with a couple of our colleagues. I will stay long enough to brief them on what has happened, then ask Vesper to conduct the rest of the meeting so you won't be left on your own for more than a few minutes. Here is my pager number, just in case." She hands me a business card.

They gather up their laptops and files, and then they're gone, leaving me, a premed student, alone with the six subjects. This has got to be breaking about a million hospital policies. I guess it shows exactly how desperate Zhu and Vesper are. They could have at least left an EMT with me, but I remember that Zhu only plans on being gone for a few minutes. I think that at this point everyone is so panicked that rationality has been thrown out the window.

I gaze around the low-lit room at the sleepers fanned out around the Tower like living corpses. Red and green diodes flicker on and off, spilling threads of colored light across the bodies, creating the impression of movement.

I will not get creeped out. I will not get creeped out.

I pull out the test file and flip back to trial subject seven. Zhu and Vesper keep bringing him up, and I remember one of them referring to him at the beginning of the test as a *wild card*. I let my curiosity take over, and quickly become absorbed in a story so horrific that I forget about everything else except a boy named Brett Alighieri.

Scrawled in large letters across the top of his file are the words "Fatal Familial Insomnia." An informational sheet stapled to the first page defines FFI as a very rare inherited disease that results in a rapid and lethal deterioration of the brain, comparable to mad cow disease. It only affects forty families worldwide, but if one parent carries the gene, their offspring have fifty percent chance of inheriting it and developing the disease. So basically, if you happen to be born into one of those forty families, you're screwed.

The following notes were written by Zhu herself. She was the one who diagnosed Brett and remained the specialist overseeing his case. I get out my pen and note:

- *FFI's symptoms don't usually show up until middle age.*
- *By the time Brett's grandfather died of FFI and his family discovered what it was, his mom already had five kids.*

- *She tested positive for FFI, but the kids (all under the age of twenty) chose not to be tested.*

I put down the file and think of what that means. I imagine, at my age, being offered a test that will tell me if I'm going to die from a horrible brain-degenerating disease in the next twenty years. Fifty percent chance I don't have it and can live my life normally. But fifty percent I do, and I'll be obsessing about it until I get sick and die. Do I spend those years single or get together with someone who's going to have to watch me die? Not even to mention having kids . . . who would be born with a fifty percent chance of having the disease too. Is ignorance bliss, or just stupidity? I honestly don't know if I would agree to the test either.

I rub my forehead and keep reading. Brett started showing signs of sleep disturbances around his eighteenth birthday. His parents weren't worried right away—he was too young to develop FFI. But when his insomnia rapidly grew worse, they brought him to the Pasithea Facility, and Zhu diagnosed him with FFI. It was just two days after his eighteenth birthday. He was one of the youngest people to have ever been diagnosed.

Within weeks, he had difficulty walking and began to slur. He moved from home to an inpatient room in the hospital.

Zhu documented Brett's decline in detail: while he was unconscious, he made movements like combing his hair, buttoning up his shirt, and eating with an invisible fork and knife. He was living in a permanent state of presleep behavior, unable to go deeper.

I read how the disease typically progresses, and realize it's one of the scariest ones I've ever come across. Victims go from increasing insomnia resulting in paranoia and phobias, to hal-lucinations and panic attacks, then complete inability to sleep, accompanied by rapid weight loss, and dementia, at which point they become unresponsive or mute.

Death soon follows.

No cure for FFI has ever been found. The death rate is *one hundred percent.*

At month nine of the disease, Brett had reached the hal-lucinatory stage. Half the time he thought he was some sort of tentacled alien, and the other half he had no idea who or where he was. And he had begun losing weight. The majority of victims die around eighteen months. This test was to be his last hope. A shot in the dark, from what it sounded like, but at least it was something.

I swivel my chair around and look at the boy lying on bed seven. He is gaunt and sickly looking. Now I understand the conversations Zhu and Vesper were having during the first few minutes of the test . . . before disaster struck. No wonder they were so excited that he had passed into REM sleep with the other subjects after the five brief rounds of electrical pulses. For them, it must have seemed like a miracle.

This boy who had barely slept for nine months had actually gone into REM sleep. Might still be sleeping now, if my hunch is right. If it weren't for the brain waves, Zhu and Vesper might believe it too.

Something occurs to me. What if the brain waves aren't actually delta at all? What if, when the electrical current went berserk, it created brain waves that are different enough from regular REM and NREM states that they can't be measured by a traditional EEG monitor?

What if I am becoming completely delusional? I thought-check myself. Who am I to be coming up with these crazy theories when the experts themselves don't have a clue what's going on?

But a small, nagging voice prods me: *It's exactly because you don't have their experience that you're not blinded by their presuppositions. You're able to think outside the box.*

Shaking my head, I shut the voice out. Because at the end of the day, it doesn't matter. There's nothing I can do. The one time I tried to talk to Vesper about it, he shot me down so fast that I wasn't even able to respond. I'm not brave or stupid enough to try something like that again.

I look at the timer I've set on my desktop. *Shit.* Zhu and Vesper have been gone for thirty minutes. I open my Gmail to find a message from Hal entitled, *You're not going to believe this.*

I read it in a state of shock. A shiver travels down my spine as I look up at my monitor at the immobile form of the boy lying on bed four. It could mean nothing. It could mean everything. It cannot mean anything good.

CHAPTER 26

FERGUS

I'M FALLING WITH THE STATIC MONSTER CREA-
ture wrapped around me. We hit the ground hard, and I feel a
bone in my upper arm break with a crunch and a knife of pain
stab my shoulder. Tears spring to my eyes as I roll onto my back
and cradle my arm against my chest.

I glance around to get my bearings. We're still in the cathedral.
It's the marble floor under the dome that I hit with all my weight.

To my right, the static monster rolls a couple of times, and
then, scrambling back to its feet, lurches toward the black wall.
He reaches it just as it dissolves, and lets out a howl of despair.
Throwing himself into the space where the Wall was, he flashes
between a tentacled monster and what actually looks like a boy,
now that I have time to really look. A boy about my age. His
eyes look as mad as the homeless guy that sits outside the art

supply store Mom goes to in Manhattan.

I pull my gaze away and try to shove past the pain for an explanation of what just happened. It didn't feel like an attack. When he latched on to me, it felt like he was trying to climb me—to get back up to the rope and through the black wall. He was using me to try to get into the Void. Why?

Now that the monster no longer seems like a threat, I stagger to my feet and look around. Just yards away from us is the body of the monk I knocked off of the walkway way up in the dome: Cata's dad. The statues are grouped around it. I can't tell what they're doing to it, and I don't think I want to know. They don't seem to notice us until the static monster's loud keening attracts their attention. One by one they turn to focus on it, and then on me.

A couple of the statues—the homeless-looking one and a woman carrying what looks like a pair of stone eyes on a plate—break off from the others and head my way. My arm is killing me, and every step I take away from them shoots off a flare of pain, every movement its own slice of torture. But they're gaining on me, so however painful it is, I have to make a run for it.

Then, with a garbled roar, the static monster throws himself in front of me, writhing in his channel-surfing-quick changes between man and beast. His left arm dangles by his side, dripping blood on the cathedral floor. That's where George hacked him with the grave-digging pick, and from the look of it she did some serious damage.

He looks so unnatural, so twisted and freakish, that even the statues don't seem to know what to do with him. I take advantage of their confusion and stay hidden behind him, backing up to one of the side walls. The monster matches my retreat step by step, shielding me from the animated sculptures. We arrive at one of the niches that was abandoned—a depression carved out of the wall a few feet off the ground, large enough to fit a man-sized statue. I climb up into it, press my back against the wall, and allow the static monster to block me with his jittering form.

From behind him it looks like he's almost sizzling, popping with electricity as he morphs from one unrecognizable being to another. He always seems to come back to the form of a man, though, no matter what other forms he takes: the octopus alien I've seen before, a creepy rooster-looking thing, a skeleton with barely any flesh connecting the bones. His jerky electrical movements remind me of a film we saw in science class showing how stimulus jumps between nerve endings. Or maybe it was synapses firing in the brain.

The two statues stand on the other side of him, hissing and baring their fangs, tears of blood running down their stone cheeks. The monster seems to be protecting me, but why?

"Hello?" I call.

The thing takes a break from swiping at the statues and looks at me with multiple eyes. There is something human in there. I can see it.

"Who are you?" I ask.

It stares at me a good moment, eyes changing form and color every second like a slide show on speed, then turns his attention back to the statues. Over his shoulder, he groans the same word he's said before: "Red." But this time it sounds more like *bread.* What's that supposed to mean?

As I crouch in my saint's niche, watching this freaky monstrosity guard me from man-eating sculptures, I wonder why he has appeared in each of our dreams. What's he been doing the whole time? I try to remember when I've seen him: in the slime cave, just before we went through the Wall; by the Wall in the middle of Remi's desert; while we were digging up the coffin in the graveyard; and here in the cathedral . . . right before the Wall showed up. He's been trying to get into the Void this whole time. But why?

Since he never showed up in the Void, he must be traveling directly from nightmare to nightmare.

That thought leads me directly to the predicament of how the hell I'm going to get out of here and back with the others. Will I be stuck here, huddling behind the static monster until he runs out of energy, and then get eaten by a marble homeless guy and a girl carrying her eyes on a plate?

No. If he's traveling from dream to dream, he should be able to get into the next one. I'll just have to hope I'm able to follow him.

The two statues finally decide to attack, surging forward, trying to get past the static monster. I duck down, shielding my head defensively, forgetting about my broken bone. I scream in pain, and shove myself into the curve of the niche, squatting and cursing as I cradle my arm.

The statues swipe out at the static monster, but he moves so fast they lose their footing and stumble around in their stop-motion stiffness. Homeless guy finally rips a hole in the monster's other arm, which begins dripping blood, but it doesn't look as bad as what George did with the pick.

The eyeless woman closes in, letting out an eerie shriek, but is thrown backward by the force of the thing, whipped away by its tentacles as if by a giant blender. Homeless guy suffers the same fate, and is thrown several yards back, splintering into pieces when he hits the ground. This has, however, caught the attention of the rest of the statues, who, one by one, turn and begin making their way toward us. If they attack all at once, at least some of them will get through. I'd better be ready to fight those he doesn't throw aside with his spinning blender action.

My arm is throbbing so painfully that I finally rip off my shirt and tie it like a tourniquet as tightly as I can around the spot that hurts. Tears of pain stream down my face as I struggle with the cloth, but finally, using my teeth and my good hand, I'm able to maneuver it into a good, tight knot and the pain subsides a little.

I rub my tattoo for comfort, thinking that I'm finally in a place where I don't have to worry about a cataplectic attack. I've gone so far past fear that my senses are dulled. Nothing can scare me any more than it already has, and I'm certainly not going to laugh. The Dreamfall seems to have cured me, at least temporarily.

Crouching down, I ready myself for the oncoming attack. Just then, I hear something I never thought I would actually welcome, but when I do my heart makes a hopeful leap. It is the knock of an invisible fist on a wooden door.

The static monster looks up and around, searching for the same blue lights that I am. The fluorescent lights flicker a short distance to our right. As the second knock sounds, the wooden door materializes between the blue lines. The monster looks around at me, and I climb down from my hiding place to the marble floor, cradling my injured arm in my good hand. The two of us shuffle closer to the door, keeping an eye on the statues that watch us as if ready to pounce. As the third knock comes, the door swings open, and the wind surrounds us, tipping over vases of dead flowers and blowing piles of abandoned purple veils across the floor.

This time I move purposefully toward the door, not even waiting for the hurricane to force me through. I lose sight of the static monster in my rush to escape this nightmare and enter whatever comes next. The wind catches me up and sucks me over the threshold and into the dark.

This time, awareness comes slowly. There is an intense pressure on my chest. My vision swims as I become slowly aware of two large yellow eyes staring down at me. They have vertical irises, like a cat. I blink a couple of times. The eyes blink back. The head shifts mechanically to the side, regarding me from an angle.

The face is a shiny, oily white, but is so close to my own that I can't focus until it pulls back and widens its eyes, as if surprised. The red ball nose, the painted-on eyebrows, the oblong of red paint outlining the lips ... My consciousness finally clicks in and I recognize what is kneeling on my chest.

And as the lips spread, the clown bares a set of rotting teeth at me. It grabs the skin on either side of my jawline as if my face is made of dough and not flesh and bone. It digs its nails under my skin, and I scream in pain as it lowers its eyes to mine and hisses, "Are you ready for a facelift?"

CHAPTER 27

CATA

WE ARE STANDING IN DARKNESS, ARM LINKED IN arm, the circle we made in the Void unbroken.

"Where are we?" Remi asks softly. Before anyone can answer, there is a loud popping noise and a floodlight flashes on from high above us, angling down to illuminate our group. I hold up my arm to shield my eyes from the blinding whiteness.

"Ladies and gentlemen, do we have a show for you today!" comes a nasal voice through a loudspeaker. "Death-defying feats of bravery! Breathtaking spectacles of skill! Tonight and tonight only we plan to thrill, chill, and possibly even kill. And now for some madcap performances by your favorite merrymakers"—the voice lowers to a sinister growl—"the clowns."

A tinny-sounding circus tune blares out of invisible speakers at a painful volume as a dozen spotlights click on, sweeping the circumference of the circus ring to follow a troupe of circus clowns riding unicycles. Though there are no spectators under the big top, the clowns wave wildly at the empty bleachers. One of them honks a horn as a signal, and half peel off and head in the opposite direction, weaving expertly in and out of each other's paths. They fake near-crashes and wobble dangerously before righting themselves as they pedal around the ring.

"Is this your dream, Ant?" I yell over the deafening music.

"Yes," he says. His face is almost as white as the clowns. A lump forms in my throat as I witness his panic.

"What happens?" Sinclair calls from Ant's other side.

"They put on a show and try to kill everyone," the boy responds, wide eyes trailing the clowns' trajectory.

"Kind of figured it was something like that," Sinclair says, licking his lips nervously.

We have stayed in our circle formation but face outward now, grouped together defensively.

The clowns are riding progressively closer to us, and are swinging lassos around their heads. They are making cowboy noises—*yee-haw* and *giddyap*—spinning the lassos until, all at once, they throw them and suddenly I can't move. My arms are pinned down to my sides, and as the lasso tightens around me, I'm jerked off my feet, stumbling backward out of the harsh glare of the floodlight.

The clowns have abandoned their unicycles and are walking each one of us on the end of their rope. "Why don't you take a load off," screeches my captor, loud enough for an audience to enjoy, and from nowhere he produces a wooden chair that he shoves me into. He slips the lasso over the back of the chair and wraps the rope around and around until I am immobilized. After tying it off into a knot, the clown leans in close to my face, giving me a clear view of him for the first time.

He looks like the clown from that Stephen King book. A bald wig with red fuzzy hair glued to the back and sides, evilly stenciled eyebrows, red rubber nose. As he smiles, he reveals sharp yellow teeth. "You're going to enjoy this show," he says in the deranged voice of a clown from one of those old children's television series—the ones broadcast before programmers realized how scary kids really thought clowns were. "I just know you'll love it. Especially the ringmaster!"

As he flings his arm back to gesture toward a dark corner of the ring, a light flickers on and off, until finally it holds steady, illuminating a tall, thin clown in a top hat. Strings are attached to the clown's arms, legs, and head, hanging down from the darkness at the top of the tent. His limbs flail around like a marionette. Black lines are drawn from either corner of his lips down to his jawline, making him look like a ventriloquist's dummy.

"Our first show tonight will be the high wire," he says, his mouth randomly falling open and snapping shut, unsynchronized with the words coming through the speakers. "Come on, little boy. Take it away!"

The rope pulls the marionette clown's arm up, and his white-gloved hand points to a wire suspended between two wooden posts high above the ground. A white-faced clown is wrestling with Remi on one of the platforms leading to the wire. "I can't!" Remi yells. "I'm scared of heights."

"Then this should help," the clown retorts. He jerks Remi's head back with one hand and ties a blindfold around his eyes.

"No!" Remi screeches as the clown shoves him forward. The boy stumbles, his foot catching the wire purely by chance, and he windmills his arms to get his balance.

"There's not even a net!" I scream at the ringmaster. "Get him down from there!"

"Oh, he'll get down, all right," says the marionette. "Sooner rather than later, from what it looks like!"

Holding his head erect, Remi shuffles forward, inch by inch. It's amazing he hasn't fallen yet, but it's obvious he won't make it far.

"Need some help, little boy?" asks the clown watching him from the platform, arms crossed impatiently. Pressing his oversized shoe on the wire, he gives it a bounce.

Remi screams and topples over, twisting and flailing and somehow catching the wire under both arms. He hangs there precariously for a second before whipping one hand up and ripping the blindfold from his head, and grabbing back on to the wire for dear life.

"Don't let go!" George screams.

Remi hangs immobile for a moment, and then, summoning all of his strength, he swings one leg out and over the wire so that he's straddling it and lying along it on his belly. His legs twist around the wire, his hands grasping it firmly, and forehead pressed to it for balance.

"Well, that was boring!" announces the clown on the platform and, grabbing on to a rope hanging from the pillar next to him, swings down to the sawdust-covered ring floor.

"Keep holding on, Remi," I yell. "We'll get you down!"

The clowns find this hilarious, and bend over in exaggerated laughs, slapping their knees and holding their bellies.

"Our next show will be provided by more of our courageous volunteers," says the mouth of the ringmaster. "Bring in the beast!" A cage the size of my bedroom materializes in the middle of the ring, its metal bars rusty and bent. My clown appears in front of me holding a large butcher knife. Laughing evilly, he moves behind me. I frantically arch my neck to see what he is doing. He swings the knife high into the air, its blade flashing silver in the spotlight, and then brings it down, slicing through the ropes binding me to my chair.

I leap up and begin to run, toppling the chair over and stumbling in my effort to get away, but the clown catches me. Holding the knife to my throat, he says, "That's no way to behave as the star of the featured act!" The blade nicks my skin, and I feel blood trickle down my neck.

He shoves me forward, his large floppy shoes flanking my Converse as he thrusts me across the ring and through the open door of the cage. A second later, Sinclair joins me, thrown in by his own gleeful clown.

The creepy circus music starts back up, and a string of horses prance out of the darkness to pace around the edge of the ring.

On the back of each horse, a clown balances, waving at the empty bleachers with one hand and holding the reins with the other. The horses are a horror: emaciated, lifeless, with dull fur hanging from protruding bones. They clop wearily around the ring once, before exiting from where they entered: into the dark.

The macabre circus music stops and is replaced by a drumroll.

"Ant!" I call. "What's coming?"

Ant and George sit side by side, bound to their chairs, on the far side of the cage from the ringmaster.

"Tiger. Lion. I'm not sure," Ant says mournfully.

We don't have to wait long to find out. Three clowns grimacing grotesquely enter the ring with a tiger on a leash. The large cat is as emaciated as the horses were. I glance at Ant. So this is what fills his nightmares: abused animals, murderous clowns, and powerlessness in the face of evil. For a kid who seems to have major control issues, this seems like a worst-case scenario.

One clown walks the tiger like it's a dog, while the other two flank it, cracking whips at the pitiful beast to keep it moving. They swing open the cage door with a flourish, unclip the leash from the collar, shove the tiger in, and slam the door behind it, jumping with glee and high-fiving as they complete their task.

Sinclair and I back into a far corner of the cage. At first it seems like the tiger doesn't see us. It paces slowly from one side of the cage to the other, watching the door like it hopes it will spring open on its own. Finally, when it realizes that's not going to happen, it stops, sniffs the air, and slowly turns toward us.

The tiger's ribs jut out, its mangy fur falling into the furrows between the bones. Its eyes bulge, too large for its face, and the sadness that seemed to sedate it dissipates as it recognizes prey. The eyes narrow, the chops draw back, and it bares its flesh-ripping teeth. It seems to be channeling its hatred for its captors into the gaze it directs toward us as it growls in a terrifyingly low rumble. A sharp ridge of striped fur rises on its back as it crouches, compacting its body into a concentrated ball of fury, tail whipping back and forth as it prepares to spring.

"Knives," Sinclair whispers. I remember that the dagger Ant made for us is attached to the belt around my waist. Moving as imperceptibly as I can, I reach for the sheath and carefully pull the blade free.

Sinclair is holding his dagger in front of his face like a warning to the tiger. But the image of handsome Sinclair and his small blade confronting this enormous wild animal is ridiculous. It's not even a contest.

Sinclair doesn't seem to realize this, though, and as the beast springs, a strangled yell escapes his throat, and he lunges toward the animal. In my terrified state, it seems like one of those Japanese action movies where both fighters leap in slow motion, exchange a blow in midair, and then land, just as slowly, on opposite sides of each other, throwing sawdust into the air as they come back to earth. When the air clears, Sinclair has a four-claw scratch down one side of his face. Blood drips from it in bright red beads. On the other side of the cage, the tiger limps from a wound to its front leg.

A small voice comes from outside the cage. "Don't hurt the tiger!" Ant yells.

"Don't hurt the tiger?" Sinclair exclaims. "If we don't hurt the tiger, it's going to fucking kill us!"

I turn to see Ant crying, struggling against the ropes pinning his arms down to his sides. George sits bound beside him, trying to talk him down.

The tiger turns its attention to me, and a rush of pure fear numbs my face and makes my fingertips sting like they're being pricked by needles. *Don't dissociate,* I think, but I don't need this self-reminder. I dissociate when I feel powerless in a dangerous situation. That isn't the case here. I can do something. This time I have the power . . . and the means . . . to hurt my aggressor. But I look into the face of the tortured tiger and I choose not to use it.

"Sinclair," I say. "Let's just try to escape. If we can work together to slip past the tiger, maybe we can get out the door."

He looks like he's thinking. "I'll get the tiger to come this way," he says. "You make a run for the door."

"Okay," I agree. "Once I'm out, I'll go to the far end and try to lure it in that direction so you can have a shot for the door."

"Deal," he says, and going into this stupid-looking action-hero crouch. He makes a waving-forward gesture with his fingers, like the tiger's some kind of thug that he's going to fight in the school parking lot. The tiger looks from Sinclair to me and back. There's a deranged look in its eyes: it's probably mad from hunger.

"Hey, tiger," Sinclair calls. "Come on. Come get me." He

flashes his knife around. The glint of the metal in the circus spotlights catches the animal's attention and it lunges without even pausing to crouch and spring like it had before. I'm so shocked that I hesitate a second, but then I hear George scream, "Run, Cata!" and I throw my body across the space of the cage toward the door, ignoring the sounds of the struggle behind me.

I hurl myself onto the door, pushing with all my might. The rusty hinges groan as it opens just wide enough for me to slip out. Leaving it ajar, I sprint around to the far corner of the cage in time to see Sinclair tear himself away from the animal. His left arm hangs by his side, blood streaming from his shoulder. He grasps the knife in his right hand and slumps slightly, breathing heavily as the tiger retreats, readying for its next attack.

"Sinclair!" I yell from outside the bars. "The door is open. Go!" And then I stick my arm with my dagger through the bars and wave it around, yelling for all I'm worth to catch the tiger's attention. The animal looks stunned for a moment, then takes a couple of steps toward me.

But instead of going for the door, Sinclair runs toward the animal, grabs a tuft of mane, yanks its head back, and pulls the knife across its throat. Blood sprays across my face, blinding me.

My muscles seem to dissolve and I fall limp to the ground. Screams come from behind me, cries of horror from Ant and George. I use my shirt to wipe the tiger blood from my eyes and stare aghast at Sinclair. He releases the tiger's head and watches it slump to the floor.

"Why did you do that?" I shriek.

"What?" Sinclair says, looking confused. "I just saved us."

"You didn't have to kill it!" I cry. "The door was open. You could have gotten out."

"It doesn't matter anyway," Sinclair yells back at me. "It's just a dream!"

We are interrupted by the arrival of the three clowns who had led the tiger into the ring. They flop up to the cage in their giant shoes and freakish smiles, clapping slowly, and swing the door wide to let Sinclair step out. One of them holds Sinclair's injured arm up in the air. "Bravo!" the clown sneers.

Sinclair slashes at him with the knife, but the clown is faster and jumps out of the way while his two companions grab Sinclair by the arms, shove a chair under him, and tie him down.

"You've just won yourselves a front-row seat for the next show," the clown says, and then, pointing to me, snaps his fingers, and in a split second I go from lying in the sawdust to sitting tied to a chair next to Sinclair.

Suddenly remembering Remi, I look up to the high wire to see that the boy has shuffled his way back to the platform and is watching us with wide eyes.

A spotlight flicks on, illuminating the puppet ringmaster. "Ladies and gentlemen, what a show that was!" says the nasal voice, as he walks toward us with exaggerated movements, strings moving his knees up and down to propel him forward. He claps a congratulatory hand on Sinclair's shoulder. "This is the kind of hero every crowd loves."

"You're sick! You're all sick!" I scream at the grotesque

ringmaster, and struggle against the ropes binding me to the chair. The string holding his head slackens, lowering his face toward mine.

"*Sick*. That's a funny word," the voice says as the jointed mouth flaps, but the creature stares at me with an intensity that sends a shiver through my spine. There's something familiar about those sea-green eyes. From beneath the velvet top hat spills chin-length black hair. And inked on the inside of the forearm is a Gothic-lettered tattoo reading "DFF."

"Fergus!" I gasp. "Oh my God, you're alive!"

"Alive?" he murmurs, as if it's a word he's never heard. His face is unrecognizable: It's the pasty white, painted-on face of every circus clown that ever existed, but there's something wrong with it. It looks lumpy, like white dough has been pushed and pressed onto his skull in a haphazard manner. It looks like a face transplant. It *is* a face transplant, I realize with horror.

Unlike before, with the mouth flapping open and shut while the voice came from elsewhere, now it's Fergus's lips, not his jaw, that move. With great effort, he squeezes out a breath. "Help me," he wheezes.

"It's Fergus!" I yell, and strain against the cords binding my chest.

Immediately, his head is yanked up and one arm raises. He points a white-gloved hand toward our left where Ant and George had been sitting, and as his mouth flaps open and shut, the voice over the loudspeaker announces, "And for the final show, we have a thrilling display of death-defying knife throwing!"

A spotlight shines down on George, whose wrists and ankles are manacled to a round wooden target propped upright in the sawdust. She is dressed in a skimpy green outfit—like a one-piece bathing suit but made of shiny satin lined with black fringe—and is wearing a headpiece crowned with big green feathers.

Facing her is Ant, who is being restrained by two clowns. A third clown stands aside, brandishing a handful of knives. Ant thrashes, yelling, "No, I won't do it!"

"It seems like we're having a bit of a technical difficulty, ladies and gentlemen," puppet Fergus says, taking an exaggerated step away from me toward the clowns. "I think we're going to have to use some persuasion here to convince our knife thrower to cooperate."

One of the clowns raises a hand and flourishes Ant's notebook and pen. He holds them up high above his head. "Would anyone enjoy a magic show?" he asks in a voice that sounds like he's been inhaling helium. He points a finger and the objects explode in a flash of light. A stream of smoke wafts upward in the harsh light of the spotlight as Ant gapes in shock.

"Maybe our brave knife thrower is ready to throw," Fergus puppet says.

"I won't!" Ant screams, red-faced.

"Assistants, more encouragement, please?" The clown holding Ant forces his hands forward as the other clown peels off the fingerless gloves. Ant thrashes and begins to tap his fingers even though there is no surface for them to touch. It looks like he's doing Morse code in the air. The clown holds them up above his head, and in a poof of flame, they're gone.

"And now. Are you ready to throw?" Fergus's mouth moves, and the voice booms over the speakers.

"Never!" Ant screams.

"Good sirs?" the ringmaster says.

Ant throws himself forward, breaking free from the clown restraining him for one breathless second before the clown catches him again, and digs his clawlike fingernails into Ant's arms. Ant screams in pain as blood blooms red on his skin.

The magician clown rips the hat off Ant's head and dances around with it, whirling it around in the air. Ant screams and jerks away, jumping, arms stretched upward, trying to grab the hat back from the gleeful clown. The clown who was his captor grasps at his thin cotton shirt, shredding it with his sharp clown nails and ripping it from Ant's back as the boy lunges for the hat.

The magician clown points his finger at the hat and it disappears in a flame that illuminates Ant's face as tears pour from his eyes.

No, I realize with shock. *Her* eyes.

I stare, incredulous, at the thirteen-year-old kneeling on the ground, weeping. My eyes take in the short, spiky strawberry blond hair pulled back in glittery blue barrettes and the striped sports bra and it suddenly clicks. Ant is a girl.

"Let's see if *Antonia*," the magician clown says, accentuating the name in a way that makes it clear that speaking it is meant as its own form of torture, "is ready to throw the knives!"

"No." Ant's voice is quiet, but the silence of the big top makes it resound as if it were a gong.

"Gentlemen," Fergus says, high-stepping over to where Ant is crouched, "I think we will need your assistance."

The clowns grab Ant and force her to rise. The clown with the knives places one blade in Ant's hand and closes her fingers around it. Another clown lifts her arm above her head into a throwing position. Ant isn't even looking. She stares at the ground as sobs rack her body.

"Ant," a voice says. My eyes race to George, who has been standing silently this whole time, pinnacled to the throwing board.

"Ant," she says again, and Ant drags her head upward as if it is made of lead.

"It's okay. Really," George says, and glances at where her arm is cuffed to the side. My gaze follows hers to her tattoo, and as I watch, half of the yin-yang fades and disappears.

"No," Ant weeps. "I can't. I'm not ready."

"And the first knife flies," announces Fergus, who has jiggled over to stand next to Ant.

The clown holding Ant's arm jerks it forward, stabbing her palm with his nails so that she lets go. The knife flies toward George. It lodges in her right arm, but she doesn't even flinch, her gaze fixed firmly on Ant.

"Well thrown!" crows the ringmaster. "Knife number two!"

Ant is sagging in the arms of the clown. I would think she had fainted except she raises her head to look George in the eyes as the second knife is wedged between her fingers. The clown pulls

Ant's arm back and the knife flies, lodging into George's right thigh. Streams of blood flow from where the two knives pierce her flesh, but still she doesn't move, her gaze cemented on Ant.

"You'll be fine on your own," George says calmly.

"No," Ant sobs. "I won't. I never have been. I need you. You're six. My sixth thing. My most important thing."

"Yet again, another excellent throw," comes the ringmaster's voice from the speakers. "Knife number three! Let's try for the head this time, why don't we?"

The knife-holding clown hands another knife to Ant's captor.

But something strange is happening to puppet Fergus, who has started to shudder. He's moving his arms and legs slowly back and forth, straining like he's stuck in honey, or in a giant spiderweb. The knife-bearing clown backs away in alarm. Fergus plucks a knife from his hand and, with zombielike jerking motions, slices through the strings attached to his arms and legs. He waves the knife over his head, cutting the string holding him up, slumps for a second, and then, regaining his strength, lunges toward George.

The clown holding Ant's arm swings back and lets the knife fly toward George's head. For a moment, it seems suspended in midair as clown-faced Fergus flings himself in front of George, shielding her. A trajectory that would have hit George in the forehead instead plants the knife firmly in much-taller Fergus's chest.

"Fergus!" I cry, and Ant whips her head up to look at the marionette ringmaster, shoots a questioning look back to me, and then realizes who the knife has struck.

"NO!!!!" Ant screams.

And as she thrashes violently against her clown captor, a familiar boom rings out, shaking the tent around us and rattling the empty seats.

"The Wall!" Remi yells from high up on his platform. He scrambles down the ladder toward the floor.

Fergus stands there, frozen, his clown mouth posed in an astonished O shape. The face starts melting, dripping off in big white doughy chunks, and underneath is Fergus—high cheekbones, jade eyes, light brown skin. His teeth are bared, clenched in pain. He slowly reaches up and pulls the knife from his chest, and then collapses onto the ground.

As the second boom rings out, Remi runs up behind me and starts hacking at my ropes with his dagger. To our right, stretching beyond the edges and far above the crest of the big top, the black wall appears. And as it does, the clowns begin to deflate like balloons until all that's left of them are empty piles of shoes and clothes scattered on the ground. The tiger carcass shrinks inside the cage, becoming a lump of fur and teeth and blood.

My ropes drop to the ground and Remi yells, "Go!" as he starts on Sinclair.

I fall forward out of my chair, catch myself and sprint toward the others. "Come on, you guys!" I bellow. "Quick! The Wall's going to disappear!"

Ant is stretched out on top of Fergus, weeping as George looks on, her face twisted in distress. "Ant, get up and go!" she urges. "You have to get out of here!"

"Ant, try to get Fergus to the Wall, and I'll work on getting

George down!" I yell. Taking out my knife, I drive it under the manacle holding her arm, and use it to wedge the metal away from the wood.

"Thanks, Cata, but that's not necessary." George gives me a sad smile.

I pause and look at her like she's insane. "What do you mean? I have to get you down."

She shakes her head. "It's been nice knowing you," she whispers. And then, looking down, she calls, "Ant?"

The girl raises her head to look George in the eyes.

"Take care of yourself," George says. And then she disappears, leaving only dangling manacles and bloodstains on the giant wheel.

"What the . . . ?" I yell. I glance around the circus ring, but George hasn't reappeared anywhere I can see.

"Help me with Fergus!" Ant yells, tears streaming down her face as she tries to wrap his arm around her shoulder.

"What happened to George?" I ask.

"Just help me with Fergus," Ant insists, and as the wind rises, the third boom shakes the tent so violently that it begins to cave in on one end, canvas plunging heavily toward the ground. Sawdust rises in a blinding cloud, and the spotlights crash down one by one.

Ant and I are trying to drag Fergus between us, but although he is semiconscious and mumbling, he is deadweight and we are barely moving. Sinclair and Remi run up behind us. "Ant, Remi, go!" Sinclair yells, and takes over for Ant. We lug him between us toward the Wall. Ant and Remi turn and wait for us at the edge of the darkness.

"Just go!" I yell. And as we reach them and plow with Fergus into the Void, I see the static monster out the side of my eye. It crouches by the edge of the Wall, reaching out toward us, its wails muted by the howling of the wind.

CHAPTER 28

JAIME

THERE ARE TEN MINUTES BEFORE THE SLEEPERS
enter what I'm guessing will be their next NREM cycle. I wonder
what they're going through in their dreams right now.

There's only one file I haven't read yet. I flip to subject six, a
thirteen-year-old named Antonia Gates. In her photo, she's wearing a knit hat with earflaps and looks like a boy.

Antonia goes to a charter school in Princeton, where she has
already finished all of her high-school-level requirements. It was
suggested that she begin university early, but she chose to stay in
the same school and do as many AP courses as she could before
having to "change environments and integrate into a new social
system," as her school counselor wrote.

Her IQ is 160. Holy crap. That's up there in the genius tier of
the scale. There is a full file of notes from a string of psychiatrists

and psychologists, but they are headed with a memo from Dr. Vesper. *Note: despite the multitude of differing diagnoses for Antonia, her parents are vehemently against her being referred to as having any particular DSM classification. However, it should be kept in mind that this highly intelligent child does manifest symptoms of obsessive-compulsive disorder, with obvious physical tics, as well as behaviors normally associated with autism, specifically Asperger's syndrome. She has suffered from sleep disorders for the last year, and in the past few months her insomnia has become crippling enough to recommend this trial.*

Seven . . . now six teenagers. All with their own problems. No, that word seems wrong. Challenges? Conditions?

They each have something that has either happened to them in their life . . . an external force, as far as Catalina and Remi are concerned . . . or, in the cases of Antonia, Brett, and Fergus, something affecting their brains. As for Sinclair, I don't really understand how that works. I read something recently saying that it was a genetic condition, but as far as the nature versus nurture debate, I've heard arguments for both sides.

In any case, all of these kids have something to fight against. They all have the scales tipped against them. All I can hope is that no one else dies like BethAnn did, before the group either snaps out of it on their own or the doctors figure out some way to pull them out.

My thoughts are interrupted by a motion on my monitor. It's hard to tell from here, but it looks like one of the subjects just moved. I lean closer to the screen, watching carefully.

There it goes again: it's subject two ... Fergus. The one whose feedback never went back to normal after the last cycle. His right hand has flown up to his chest. I turn around and see that he has ripped out his IV tube, which is dripping on the floor.

I jump up and start running down the stairs toward him, then, remembering what Zhu said about emergencies, scramble back up to my workstation. I flail around for the card she gave me, find it, and punch her pager number into the telephone. As soon as it registers, I slam the receiver back down and run to Fergus's side. Leaning in to look at his Tower monitor, I see that his heart rate is rising off the charts.

His eyes fly open. Holding a fist over his heart, he seems to be pulling some invisible object from his chest before his fingers open and his hand drops back down to his side.

I glance at the defibrillator. It is activated and ready to use, but I don't dare try it myself. This is a real person. A living, breathing human being, not the test dummy I used in ER class. I look toward the door, but there's no sign of Zhu.

My heart is beating so fast, my rate is probably right up there with Fergus's. His eyes grow wider, and as he glances around the room in panic, his gaze lands on me. "Help me," he wheezes.

"Fergus, can you hear me?" I ask.

He nods, and then asks in a choked voice, "Did BethAnn make it?"

Time stops as I realize what his question means. Fergus knows something happened to BethAnn. The subjects are in there together, wherever "there" is. They are in a state of consciousness

256

that doesn't show up on regular brain-wave monitoring. They are in each other's dreams.

I snap back into myself. "BethAnn . . . She died."

Fergus squeezes his eyes shut. "It's the dreams," he says. "They're killing us."

"You're here now," I say. "You're safe."

He pauses, thinking, then shakes his head. "No, I can't leave them there. I can see it . . . the Void. You're fading and it's getting clearer. I think . . ." He sighs and lifts his hand to his heart. "I have to go back."

What? I think, my thoughts racing. *Is he hallucinating, or going back into the coma, or . . . dying?*

"Listen, Fergus." I barely knowing what I'm doing, but feel like I have to tell him what happened. "There was an accident during the test, and now the doctors think you're all in a coma. They're figuring out how to wake you up. But until they do, you have to be careful. One of you . . ."

His focus seems to fade. Can he hear me? I lean in and whisper into his ear. But before I can finish telling him everything I want to say, Fergus's eyes fly up to the ceiling and he flatlines.

I look frantically toward the door. No Zhu. I rip open Fergus's gown, pick up the defibrillator paddles, and place them above and below the heart on the left and right, like we learned in class.

And then I stop.

What am I doing? I'm a premed student, not a doctor.

This boy is dying, a voice says from inside me.

If this doesn't work and he dies, it could be blamed on me. If I do nothing, I'm blameless.

A life is in the balance.

This could cost me my degree . . . my entry to med school . . . my career.

If you stand by and let him die, you will never forgive yourself.

This could mean ending up back in Detroit.

Better to be safe than sorry.

And then the voice inside me becomes that of my dad's. My dad, who was always proud of me, no matter what. I hear pride and amusement blend in his low baritone voice. *When have* you *ever taken the safe way?*

That is the push I need. "Come on, Fergus," I say, and standing back, making sure my body isn't touching his, I press the defibrillator's shock button.

The charge convulses Fergus's body, arching it off the bed and back down. I wait, watching his monitor, palms sweaty with nerves as I watch the line continue to travel straight across the screen. No change.

I wipe my hands on my jeans, reapply the paddles, breathe out slowly, and give him a second charge. The brain-numbing steady high note of the flatline continues unchanged.

I breathe out one more time, reminding myself to keep my hands steady before realizing that I am actually completely calm. The fact that I am doing something . . . am able to actually act instead of being a powerless bystander, has sent me into that zone I've experienced before when faced with accidents. No matter how gory the compound fracture or the amount of blood pouring from a wound, if I am able to take action, I reach a sort of levelheadedness.

Which is why I am able to follow through, even when my peripheral vision catches Zhu rushing through the door, and I hear her scream, "Jaime! What the hell are you doing? Stop right now!"

I apply the third charge, and as I lift the paddles from his chest, Fergus's heart starts beating again. Zhu races over and looks down at Fergus, then up at the monitor. She registers the flatline followed by the up-and-down zigzag of his current heartbeat, and turns slowly to face me.

That's it, I think. *I'm out of here. She's going to have my head.*

"Jaime," Zhu says, her face drawn in wonder, "you just saved that boy's life."

CHAPTER 29

CATA

ANT SITS CRUMPLED IN A HEAP ON THE UNFOR-
giving blank floor of the Void. Her torn shirt and blood-spattered
shorts have once again transformed and look brand-new. Her
hands are tucked safely in the fingerless gloves, and her hat is
back, earflaps pulled down to her chin.

She kneels next to Fergus's motionless body. He lies on his
back. The ringmaster's uniform has disappeared, and he's wearing his regular clothes, but there's a hole sliced through the chest
of his blood-soaked T-shirt, and a pool of red has formed on the
ground next to him.

Remi and Sinclair walk over from where they appeared, and
the four of us crouch around Fergus's body, watching in horror
as it starts to fade.

"No! You can't die!" sobs Ant. She throws herself across his body, arms around his neck and head on his shoulder, gluing herself to him. Like she wants to disappear along with him.

As it happened with BethAnn, the color seems to seep out of Fergus. His edges blur, and he seems on the verge of vanishing when all of a sudden, his body convulses. Ant drops her hold on him and backs away.

Ever so slowly, the color begins to return. Fergus solidifies before our eyes. The steady up-and-down movement of his chest is our proof that he is not dying. He is not gone. We wait, speechless, unsure of what to expect.

As we watch, the blood dries and then disappears. The T-shirt seems to repair itself, the edges slit by the knife pulling together and reknitting. Sinclair leans over and pulls up the hem of the shirt, exposing Fergus's chest. His skin is smooth—no stab wound in sight.

Fergus's eyes flutter open and he glances around at all of us. It takes him a moment to realize where he is, and then he gives Ant a weak smile. "Hey," he breathes, "you've got a pretty powerful throwing arm."

"It wasn't me. I-I-I didn't mean . . ." she stammers, but he shakes his head.

"I know. It was the evil clowns from your dream, which, I have to say, beat all of the rest of our nightmares by miles for sheer freak factor." He slowly, haltingly props himself up on one elbow and looks around our group. "Where's George?" he asks.

Ant squeezes her eyes shut and taps three times on the floor. She takes a deep breath and then, staring at the ground, says, "George wasn't real."

"What do you mean she wasn't real?" I ask as a flush of horror sweeps up my spine.

"George . . . Georgina . . ." Ant looks around at us, measuring our reactions before continuing. "She was kind of this fictional companion I've had since I was young." She hesitates before continuing in a tone that sounds almost shy. She's forcing herself to talk . . . like a normal person. "George was the girl I always wished I could be: cool, brave, able to talk without sounding like a walking dictionary."

"Are you telling us that George was your . . . imaginary friend?" Sinclair sounds like he's about to burst into laughter. But, after a cautionary look from me, he contains himself and crosses his arms, creasing his face with an expression of concern.

"I never thought she was real," Ant responds. "But when she appeared here in the Dreamfall, well, it was so nice to have her actually be able to take care of me that I didn't say anything."

"None of us would have believed you anyway," I reassure her.

"So everything she said . . . everything she did . . ." Fergus begins, with a look straddling embarrassment and loss.

" . . . came from my head," Ant mumbles, looking down.

I lean over to put an arm around the kid who I can't help but still think of as a boy. *Like it even matters.* Fergus sits up and presses a hand to his forehead.

We are all silent, the others surely doing what I am: trying to remember everything that had happened with George since we got here. Trying to reconcile the fact that she and Ant were the same person.

"Wait, that doesn't make sense," Remi says finally. "There are supposed to be seven of us."

Fergus stares at him, confused.

I explain. "In the last Void, when you weren't here, we were discussing what you said about us all having sleep disorders. And we remembered about being asked to participate in this clinical trial to cure our insomnia. Something that included electroconvulsive therapy."

"Which explains our memory loss," adds Sinclair.

A look of amazement and then comprehension comes over Fergus's face. "Oh my God, I was just there!" he exclaims.

"Where?" Remi asks.

"In the lab where the trial is taking place . . . the room where all our bodies are lying."

"What?" "What do you mean?" "How could . . ." We all speak at once.

"In the circus, after I got stabbed and went unconscious, I woke for a moment somewhere else. It was this clinical-looking place, and I was lying down, attached to all of these monitors. Cata, you were on a bed to my right. The one to my left was empty. There were other beds, all grouped around a computer we're hooked up to—blinking lights, heartbeat monitors, the works.

"And there was this person there, leaning over me . . . I couldn't really see who it was. They said that something went wrong with the experiment, and that the outside world thinks we're in a coma. Doctors are trying to find a way to get us out. They also said . . ." Fergus pauses and looks around at the group. ". . . that BethAnn died."

We stare at each other in shock. "Well, that answers the question about what happens if we die here," Sinclair says.

Remi speaks back up. "But what about the seven?"

"The seven what?" Fergus asks.

"Seven test subjects. There were supposed to be seven of us in the trial," Remi insists. "BethAnn, you, me, Ant, Cata, Sinclair, and George. So if George never existed, then who is the seventh subject? And why aren't they here with us?"

"Maybe they pulled out of the trial at the last moment," Sinclair ventures.

Fergus gets this horrified look on his face. "Oh my God. It can't . . ."

"What?" I ask.

He takes a moment to think. "When I fell in the cathedral, when that static monster thing pulled me off the rope, I stayed in that nightmare."

"How did you survive?" Remi asks.

"The monster. It actually shielded me from those killer statues until the time was up and we were able to go through the blue door directly into the circus nightmare. While he was protecting me, I thought about all of the times he had shown up. We thought he was trying to keep us from going into the Void. But I think he was actually trying to get into the Void himself."

There is a silence as everyone processes Fergus's words. "When I looked closely, when it wasn't shifting from one creature to the next, I saw a guy about my age. I think he's one of us," he concludes. "He's just been stuck going from nightmare to nightmare, not able to leave."

"And we've been trying to kill him," Ant says in a whisper. "We actually *might* have killed him. I saw him in the circus as we were leaving."

"So did I," I say. "He was crouching next to the Wall, not even trying to get through. He looked injured."

"What's wrong with him, then?" Remi asks. "Why do we all look like we do and he looks like a monster?"

Ant responds, "Our appearance to one another is obviously a projection of how we perceive ourselves, since our senses in the Dreamfall are processed by our minds without typical stimulation of our sensory organs."

Remi just stares, unwilling to say he doesn't understand.

"Where's George when we need a translation?" Sinclair mumbles.

"Oh my God, Sinclair!" I scold.

"It's okay," Ant says, and tries again. "Our eyes, ears, hands, mouths, and noses are back in that lab. So our minds are fabricating what we see, hear, feel, taste, and smell here. You see me as I see myself in my mind."

"So that . . . person . . . sees himself as a monster?" Remi asks.

"There must be something wrong with him," I respond, looking at Ant for her opinion. She stares at the floor until her notebook and pen appear, and begins scribbling something. No one seems to notice. *By this point, we aren't fazed by anything she does,* I think with a rueful smile.

"Maybe his brain got fried by the experiment," Sinclair offers, continuing my line of thought.

"Whatever the case," Fergus says, "we have to try to save him."

"Well, if this isn't the last nightmare, like we were hoping, then we'll have our chance to try," Sinclair concludes.

"We worked out that we've been here almost six hours—the length of time we remembered the trial was supposed to last," I explain to Fergus. "The hope was this was all just a part of the test and when it was over we'd wake up."

"Not according to what I was told in the lab," Fergus says. "It sounds like we're stuck here. We'll have to have to try to survive until the doctors find a way to get us out."

"Or we find our own way out," Ant says.

Everyone looks at her expectantly, like she might already have an answer, but she just shrugs.

"We might as well get ready," I say, trying to hide the defeat in my voice. "Does everyone still have their weapons?"

Remi is wearing his knife, sheathed, as is Ant. I have mine. Sinclair must have left his behind in the tiger's cage, where he slaughtered that poor animal. His eyes meet mine, and I can tell he knows what I'm thinking. "I saved our lives," he whispers to me defensively.

"It was unnecessary," I insist. He touches my arm, but I pull away. I'm not ready to forgive him.

"Listen, none of us have real fighting skills," Fergus says. "I agree we need weapons to defend ourselves, but someone suggested more useful objects before: rope, flashlights . . . How about a lighter for fire? They could be equally useful for survival instead of focusing only on firepower."

Remi frowns, obviously disagreeing. Sinclair just purses his lips and shrugs. Fergus stares at them, looking like he just remembered something, his brow knit in concentration.

"What?" Sinclair asks defensively.

"That person in the lab . . . They told me something strange."

"What was it?" I ask.

Fergus looks back and forth from Remi to Sinclair, over to me and Ant, and then shakes his head. "Nothing," he says, turning away and massaging his temples.

Ant walks a couple of steps away and sits in her meditation pose. As we watch, a crossbow appears on the ground in front of her, and then a short sword, a blanket, an industrial-sized flashlight, a coil of rope, and other objects that make it look like we're going on a camping trip instead of the darkest corners of each other's subconscious. She finishes with a set of five backpacks and, opening her eyes, looks up at us with an earnest expression, as if wondering if it was good enough.

"That's amazing," Fergus says, as we all stand and begin strapping weapons to us with the holsters and belts that Ant provided.

"I don't even know how to use this," Remi says, holding up the crossbow.

"From now on, this is all about survival," I say. "About keeping ourselves—and each other—alive. After this, the Void will be practice time. We'll need every minute we can get."

Ant glances up at me, and her eyes are clouded with worry and guilt.

"What is it, Ant?" I ask.

Before she can answer, Fergus lets out a groan. He looks over at me, his face reddening as he raises a hand to his chest.

"What's wrong?" I ask, rushing over to him. I put an arm around him and help him lower himself to sit on the ground. His face has turned beet red.

The others have gathered around us, and Sinclair squats in front of him, looking him in the eyes. "Are you okay, man?"

"My heart," Fergus gasps. "Something . . . wrong . . ."

"Is this one of your narcolepsy attacks?" I ask.

"No." Fergus chokes out the words, "Don't know what's wrong . . . my heart."

"Someone . . . do something!" Ant yells as Fergus's body goes limp.

Sinclair rolls him onto his back and presses his ear to his chest. "His heart's still beating."

Ant holds her fingers to Fergus's wrist. "His pulse is fast, but not dangerously so."

I place my palm in front of his mouth. "He's still breathing."

We crouch around him, staring in disbelief. And then, from all around us comes the first knock.

"Oh no. Not now!" cries Ant as the blue lights flicker on nearby. We scramble to our feet as the wooden door appears. As the second knock booms, it inches open with an ancient creak.

"Should we try to push Fergus away from the door so he won't get swept through?" Remi calls as the wind starts howling around us.

"Doesn't matter," shouts Sinclair. "I was pretty far away that one time, and it sucked me in anyway. No one stays in the Void."

"Who has the rope?" I yell. Ant rummages through her backpack and pulls out a coil of strong cord.

"Sinclair, pull Fergus up so that he's sitting." He looks at me, not understanding. "Just do it!" I yell, and as he props Fergus up, I slide down to sit behind him, my back to his.

"Tie us together," I urge. Ant has understood and is already knotting the first loop around our torsos before encircling us again and again and then tucking the loose end under the top cord.

She flops down next to me and takes my hand, and Sinclair positions himself on my other side, with Remi completing the circle between them. I lean forward, balancing Fergus's weight on my back, and, looking at the others, think of how not long ago the circle was bigger. Only hours ago, there were seven of us.

How long will our dwindling group survive? Can we hold out long enough for those outside the Dreamfall to rescue us? Or by the time they figure it out, will we all be dead?

The wind whips us around like we're as light as a daisy chain, picks us up, and thrusts us through the door. And like that, we're gone.

EPILOGUE

JAIME

I OPEN MY GMAIL AGAIN AND REREAD HAL'S chilling message.

Re: You're not going to believe this

Hacked the shrink's account, and found her file on Sinclair. Hope you're sitting down.

There were notes on the three kids' deaths . . . basically the same info as the police file. But shrink noted that the reason the police launched an investigation against Sinclair in the first place was because he behaved "erratically" when he was interviewed about the boy who got locked in the basement.

Apparently, the sick fucker laughed when the detective gave him the details of the boy's death. That raised suspicions. He was cleared, though, when his parents confirmed their family was out of town when it happened.

But get this . . . Sinclair's mom came to see the shrink on her own. She confessed that they had made up the out-of-town alibi to protect him, but that she was sure he had no involvement and wanted to spare him the "emotional trauma" of further questioning.

The shrink, however, was not convinced. She gave him this test called the Hare Psychopathy Checklist, and the dude is an off-the-charts psychopath. He's listed as showing "manipulative behavior, little or no empathy, lack of remorse or guilt, compulsive lying, grandiose self-worth," the list goes on and on.

The shrink began to suspect that he killed all three of the kids. But until he said something to prove it, she couldn't go to the police. She got him signed up for this experimental procedure to treat his insomnia and plans on "pressing him further" after he gets cured.

I saved screenshots in case you want them.

Don't know why you're checking on these people, but I
sincerely hope you never meet this guy in real life.

A shiver travels down my spine as I look at the immobile form
of the boy on my monitor. I hope that Fergus understood what I
told him before he went back under. Otherwise he and the others
could suffer the same fate as the kids from Sinclair's past.

I pray with all my heart he heard my last words: *One of you is
a psychopath.*

ACKNOWLEDGMENTS

MY BIGGEST THANK-YOU GOES TO MY EDITORS AT HarperTeen: Chris Hernandez and Tara Weikum. You saw the story when it was just an idea and grilled me (necessarily) about the details until it was actually worth writing. After that, you shepherded my wild imaginings into something that actually made sense. You both know how to push my buttons in the very best of ways.

Much thanks to the lovely Stacy Glick for ensuring that *Dreamfall* followed its predecessors into the hallowed halls of HarperTeen.

Thank you to Jenna Stempel for giving my book its spine-chilling cover, and to Alexandra Rakaczki and Janet Robbins Rosenberg for transforming my grammar from spine-chilling to presentable.

Thank you to my assistant, Kayla, for being my second brain, and for always being willing to do tasks that aren't in your job description. Like pushing me in a wheelchair past the Mona Lisa.

Merci to Lenore Appelhans and Claudia Depkin for beta-reading the manuscript and giving much-appreciated reassurance and feedback. Lenore said it bugged the hell out of her not to know if Jaime was a boy or a girl, which reassured me I was doing the right thing. Thank you to the Bear for indulging me repeatedly with the craziest of brainstorming sessions.

Thank you to my friends for your encouragement and cheerleading during the planning and writing of *Dreamfall*, including Lawrence Daly, Lori Ann Stephens, Diana Canfield, Alex Goddard, Mags Harnett, Cassi Bryn-Michalik, Marie Cambolieu, Carina Rozenfeld, Christi Daugherty, Jack Jewers, Elizabeth Fordham, and Celeste Rhoads.

Some friends were generous enough to open up their private lives for the benefit of my little horror story. Thanks to Penny Russel Janiak for explaining her experience with hypnagogic hallucinations. Also much gratitude to my author friend Bethany Hagen, who not only talked with me in-depth about narcolepsy, but let me use her scariest hallucination in the book. (The clown that kneels on Fergus's chest and rips off his face.) I hope it makes the dream worthwhile to know it's now out there, lurking between the pages and scaring readers. Thank you to my friend who underwent electroconvulsive therapy and talked to me in detail about the process and related memory issues.

Thank you, Barbara, for being there for me after Mom died. And for what came after.

Thanks to Dr. Lewis Foss for reading an early version of the book and verifying that my general medical terms and descriptions were accurate enough to be credible. And to the sleep research specialist who prefers to remain anonymous (can you blame him?) for giving me a thumbs-up on the feasibility of Pasithea Facility's practices and correcting me on the details of my teens' sleep disorders.

A shout-out to H. P. Lovecraft for inspiring the ambiance of Fergus's cave dream. I always feel slimy after reading his stories and tried to reproduce the sensation with the phlegm lake.

I owe the flayed-man dream to my sixteen-year-old self, who lay petrified in her bed in the antebellum house hearing the squishy footsteps of the flayed man and thinking, "If only I could write this down, it would be as scary as Stephen King." Oh, and thank you to Stephen King for giving me my lifelong fear of clowns.

Thank you to Ray Bradbury's *The Illustrated Man* and *The Martian Chronicles* for fitting me with special glasses that allow me to see past the normal world to the creepiness lurking behind. Thank you to Charles Williams for freaking me out with *All Hallows' Eve*. Thank you to HBO for screening *Alien* when I was fourteen and babysitting for the Freemans and was so scared I couldn't get off the couch and had to call my mom. Thank you to Vincent Price for giving me nightmares for weeks after watching *House of Wax*. Thank you to the *Twilight Zone*. Thank you to ountain Brook Elementary School for screening *The Blob* late .t night so that I had to walk back home in the dark with my sister imagining a huge red snotball oozing after us. Thank you to my pastor for screening *A Thief in the Night* in the church basement in the 1970s and demonstrating that if you scare a teenager badly enough . . . they still won't believe what you tell them.

Thank you to my kids for being so scared of weeping angels that I had to put them in Cata's dream. I also appreciate your suggestions for the nightmares based on your own dreams. Unfortunately, they were too scary to use.

And above all, thank you to my readers for your never-ending enthusiasm for my stories. You inspire me and encourage me to persevere, even when every word seems a struggle. I handed out virtual tissues for the Die For Me series and virtual crossbows for After the End. Now you all deserve a night-light.

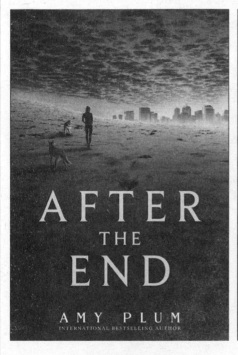
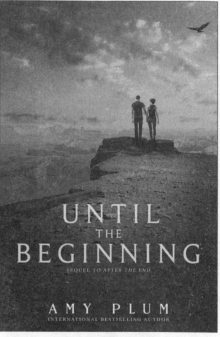

FALL IN LOVE IN PARIS

JOIN THE

Epic Reads
COMMUNITY

THE ULTIMATE YA DESTINATION

◀ **DISCOVER** ▶
your next favorite read

◀ **MEET** ▶
new authors to love

◀ **WIN** ▶
free books

◀ **SHARE** ▶
infographics, playlists, quizzes, and more

◀ **WATCH** ▶
the latest videos

◀ **TUNE IN** ▶
to Tea Time with Team Epic Reads